THE GALLOPERS

Jon Ransom

MUSWELL
PRESS

First published by Muswell Press in 2024

Typeset in Bembo by M Rules
Copyright Jon Ransom © 2024
This edition published 2025

Printed and bound by
CPI Group (UK) Ltd, Croydon CR0 4YY.

A CIP catalogue record for this book is
available from the British Library

ISBN: 9781738452873
eISBN: 9781739193034

Muswell Press
London N6 5HQ
www.muswell-press.co.uk

For Mark Craig Ackroyd

1953

Just as the moon shining in a bucket full with water isn't really the moon, I am something other than I appear to be. Something that keeps me restless. Hauled into night again and again to our field. An arrow-shaped piece of land belonging to Aunt Dreama and me. Since the flood, since that wild night when the moon was a different colour altogether, half the farmers have turned against us. The rest murmur mistruths about my mother. Who was washed away. Though I have to swallow the lies. Put my back to those who hate me. Gather the stones that boom through the windowpanes at daybreak, collected in a pile at the foot of my bed. I tell Dreama we should pack up. Move to another town. Any town. Find someplace shiny where nobody knows how cunning dirt can be. Though Dreama won't give in to the situation, or hear of quitting the field. Not now Jimmy Smart is living out in black barn stirring everything up. Fortnight past he drove Peg over from Wolferton station. Two of them arguing like crows. Her believing he almost killed them dead, them lucky not to be at the bottom of Coalyard Creek. Jimmy Smart had shrugged like it was no big thing. The whole while I'd looked on everywhere but Jimmy Smart's gaze. Might be my own would have given me away. When Peg had told Dreama windowpanes cost something, that she could do worse than let him live out there in black barn, Dreama sucked on her Woodbine for the longest time while a big bluebottle buzzed about her head. Inside my own head, I'd already seen it all. Knowing this stranger, who'd not long been hauling luggage at the station, would disrupt everything worse than the flood, a rush of water that swept over all the dirt around here but our own. Dreama sighed. Her paying Peg some debt these women had held close. She nodded towards black barn. Told Jimmy Smart where to find the fold-out bed. And that's how I find myself kneeling before this open window holding my pale dick in moon-light, while watching Jimmy Smart wash himself off outside black barn. His bare skin wet with cool water from the tin bucket. Until his white underdrawers are soaked clear. Now I'm dazed. Dizzy with desire. Rushing my palm against my mouth to stifle the groan. Afterwards, when my balls are empty and black barn quiet, I go outside. The night is still, folded all around me and the wooden planks. The air heavy against my skin. Dirt warm beneath bare feet. I dip my hand into the bucket breaking the moon into different pieces. Too many to count. Scoop up a handful and drink. Even though it's just a reflection I try to taste the moon turning around and around in my mouth. Nothing. And drift off into the field, where I put my back against the ground. Down in the coolness I tell myself I'll stay away from the mysterious showman Jimmy Smart. Keep quiet around him. Because I know not even swallowing moonlight can wash away my sissy mouth, that has gotten me into more misfortune than not.

Don't talk much, do you? Jimmy Smart says.

Not too much, I say.

Words don't start where you think they do. Or come from where you imagine. Cuz you'd be wrong in believing they slide down from your head into the back of your throat. All words run upwards from the belly, hitchhiking on your breath.

That—true?

Reckon so.

But—

Go on—

How'd they turn out—sounding the way mine do?

Mystery to me.

You mean—you don't know? I say.

It's a dilemma for sure, Jimmy Smart says.

Like a sparrow torn from the flock after a fierce wind, I worry Dreama has gone astray. Since the flood it's happened more and more. Arising as the wideness of her eyes, their blue foreseeing a sudden something invisible to me. I know the broken windowpanes are disrupting the house, and I've yet to discover whose hands hurl the stones. But I will. And when I hear a hammering below, for a moment I believe it might be yet another. Though instead of finding pieces of glass glinting, Jimmy Smart is stood at our backdoor. Breathless. Boot laces untied and bare-chested. His mouth regretful without saying a word. And when he does speak it's to tell me to bring a blanket and no more. I fetch Dreama's purple knitted shawl from the back of her chair. Tug on my boots. Trail behind the showman out to the field. He moves quick. Like he's been heading somewhere his entire life. It's more than the pace he keeps and the way he doesn't care to glance back over his shoulder. Along the way I wonder about the scar on his back, sickle-shaped and a palm wide. How it might feel beneath the tip of my forefinger. Before long we're into the field. Damp grass stirring in early light. Beyond the field and further there is a stretch of indigo mountain that isn't really there. These illusions follow Jimmy Smart around. At the centre of our field where the grass doesn't care to grow, we find Dreama stark naked. Her turning circles. Talking to ghosts. I feel bashful all of a sudden. But Jimmy Smart doesn't seem to mind, and I suppose that must be because he's seen his share of bare women. He takes the shawl from my hands and holds it out like a sail, catching her in a fold of purple. Dreama surrenders. Her gaze empty, except for the colour of cornflowers. And Jimmy Smart steers her towards the house, through the backdoor, and pulls out a chair. He wants to know if I need anything more. I shake my head, not trusting my mouth. Light Dreama a Woodbine and place it in her hand. Metallic smoke whirls about her yellow hair. And when she exhales, the shawl slips down until I can see one pale breast. Dreama is something else.

I'm not a child, Dreama says.

I know that, I say.

Then don't treat me like one.

What would you have me do?

Leave me be.

Out in the field—like that?

It's my field.

Not any longer—

You ever wonder what's after?

I never wonder that.

Eliza could come back yet.

No—my mother's gone.

I can feel her. Right here. In my chest. Like a stone,
Dreama says.

We don't need any more of them, I say.

Shane Wright's cheeks are bluish all the time. Comes from
him having coal-coloured hair beneath pale skin. The light
this day is bluish too, laid about on each and every surface.
There is blue on the Heidelberg press, that sucks and sighs
steadily. Blue steel shelves with blue tins of ink that are really
black. And stacked in wooden racks piles of printed paper a
surprising shade of indigo. Light is clever like that. I wipe

sweat from my forehead with the sleeve of my overalls. Even with every window hung open the air inside the printshop is unlike anywhere else. Heavy with the heady scent of ink on paper, set-off powder and solvent. Beneath this sweat from the men who turn everything, disturbing my nostrils. I am hypnotised by smell. Unlike light, smell gets everywhere. Underside, inside. There's nowhere it can't roam. I care for the smell of clean palms, a spent match after lighting my Woodbine, and the middle of Shane Wright's chest where his hair is thickest. Yet today I can't stand it. And tell them I'm going outside. Where I find the yard is also bluish, and this bothers me too. Dreama would claim it means something. Something more than superstition. Might be there's truth to it. As when I drift back towards that wild night and the hours beforehand, there was an odd yellowish tinge to the twilight. Something burning beneath. Even the townies talked of it in the days following the flood, when the water was black and calm. Dreama had sworn it was the same colour I turned as a newborn. Then Shane Wright is out in the yard alongside me, interrupting my thoughts. We smoke our Woodbines and watch the yard. There's nothing much to look at. Narrow and six-foot walled on either side, with a privy behind a blue door at the far end I'm considering. But if you stand still long enough you'll see pretty purple flowers spring from between red bricks. I consider bringing one home for Dreama. Though Shane Wright has other ideas. He's licked his thumb and is rubbing ink he tells me is ruining my chin. His eyes wrinkled from squinting at the sun. Stirring the situation. I forget about my need to urinate. As I've no desire to piss in my own face.

Been watching you all morning, Shane Wright says.

I know— I say.

You'll stay after then?

I can't—not today.

How come?

I promised Dreama something.

What's that then?

Nothing—important.

Heard about that showman you have living out in black barn. Don't see why he'd want to work at the station. What about his own people?

None of my concern— Suppose everyone knows he's beside our field?

Can see it'd be handy having him around.

I guess—

He have a name?

Jimmy Smart.

What's he like? Shane Wright says.

Like nobody around these parts, I say.

The iron bridge is high enough to hurl ourselves off. The water deep enough. We strip beneath the moon, bright as a dinnerplate licked clean. I fold my shirt and trousers. Jimmy Smart grins, ditches his clothes beside tall grass wild with night music. He is distracting, being bare-arsed and not bashful. Though my heart's hammering I'm glad I lied to Shane Wright about a promise I hadn't made to Dreama. That I agreed to drive out to the river with the showman. On the ride here he'd talked about the station. Working for Peg alongside her daughter, Petal. Wanted to know how far back I'd known them. Most my entire life. Way before Peg became a war widow. I told him things were troubled between the two of us. Since the flood. That's when he asked if I thought Petal was beautiful. There's no denying her beauty. Yet I don't care for it nearly so much as watching his pale backside move up the bank, all the way to the train tracks. We sidestep along the bridge and balance ourselves, toes tipping the edge. Up here the night is thick with gnats. We swipe them away. In truth I've been afraid of water since the flood washed my mother away. Yet being beside Jimmy Smart makes me feel untethered from before. It's why I'm here instead of staying away like I'd planned to. Then he wants to know if I'm set. I nod. And we leap into the night. The feeling of falling rushes over my skin lasting the longest time. Before disappearing beneath the wet, ink black and everywhere. Kicking against the cold until I'm above the surface. Hearing Jimmy Smart whoop. Him shaking the river from his hair. We hang there in the water while a freight train rolls across the track, moving sand that someday will be the windowpanes people look out of. He tells me he's cooled off now. I follow behind onto the riverbank, the grass sharp beneath my feet. No breeze at all. Using our underdrawers we wipe the wet from our skin. Pull on trousers. Shirts left unbuttoned. Lastly our boots. Jimmy Smart lights two Woodbines, passes me the spare.

When he asks about the field, how exactly is it cursed, I open my mouth but no sound comes out. I wish I could tell him the truth. I know what Dreama would say—if wishes were horses. He looks at me for a time, his eyes like two pieces of shiny black flint I can see myself in.

Go ahead and ask me. Cuz I can see you've something on your mind, Jimmy Smart says.

How'd you know—'bout the curse? I say.

Petal told me the field's no good.

She's right.

Looks fine to me. Like the flood water went around it.

Some things are not—what they seem.

Those broken windowpanes have anything to do with it? Cuz if I catch the bastard hurling stones he'll be sorry.

The stones started—after the flood.

If you're right about the curse, I know a fortune teller who might know how to rid you and your aunt of it. Name's Esme. She's not blood or nothing. Closest thing I have mind. And she knows things no one else can.

Like what?

I don't know. If it'll rain tomorrow.

Will it?

You'd have to ask her.

She tell you—your future?

Don't need no one to tell me that, Jimmy Smart says.

Me neither, I say.

Dreama has gone to church. I won't believe there's anything inside those walls that'll ease her. Not the Reverend, who is a liar. Not Jesus, hanging nearly naked tormenting me. All church brings is more trouble. Her returning home with an armload of remnants the flood left behind. Strewn beside fields where crops can't grow now the dirt's ruined. Mismatched shoes. A child's doll. Half a plate, crescent-shaped and more blue than white. And cabinet photographs of stiff people who appear conjured from another time. Yet it's more. I'm mad at Dreama and God and Jimmy Smart for stirring something inside I haven't any name for. Mostly I'm mad at myself. Desire is cunning like that. While I patch our windowpane with greaseproof paper I can see him through the hole. Standing idle. He's handsome in the same way Petal and Dreama are beautiful. My mother too. These women who make men ache after them. I press my left eye against the glass and squint through the hole. Like being fourteen years old at the seashore when I held on to the coin-operated telescope. Inside the circle a gang of five men were fooling around. Their skin tan. Hair glinting in bright sunlight. But blackness came as my money ran out, and I'd been left with nothing but big white gulls overhead swooping and calling *huoh-huoh-huoh*. Ladybirds that crawled up and down my arms no matter how hard I brushed them away. A red-faced man on the platform told us they blew in the day before. Thousands of them. Until the sand was plagued with their black and red backs. Dreama told me it meant trouble's coming. I nodded because it was too sweltering to be disagreeable. And the picnic bag heavy to haul across the shoreline, until we found a stretch of sand near the swell with hardly any stones. The waves roared, their tips like torn paper, before they rushed up and soaked away. Unbuttoning my shirt, I told Dreama and my mother I was going in. The water, more green than blue, grew colder the further I waded. Until I was alongside the herd of men from the telescope. Only they were older up close. Skin pock-marked out from behind sand-worn glass. Still they stirred me. I ducked beneath the wet and when I surfaced they'd moved further away. Turned back and laughed at me. I wished a whale would swallow them. And swam back to shore. There I'd ate warm sandwiches with my mother and Dreama. Until restlessness pulled me down the beach, towards the cliffs, coloured red as rust. Beside a rockpool where sticklebacks darted about, I reached in my hand and disturbed them. Unaware I'd been followed. Until his shadow turned the water stormy. He was one of the men from before. A gap between his front teeth. His swimming trunks bright blue, except for the ladybirds. Though he didn't utter a word, I knew he wanted me to go with him. I trailed behind. Watched muscles move beneath summer skin. At the foot of the cliff he disappeared. Behind a fallen rock, high as our heads, I found him with his swimming trunks heaped at his ankles. While he'd tugged his dick, straightening the kink. My own dick had been rigid since the rockpool. He put his palms either side my head and lowered me down.

11

Then my nose was busy with the smell of him. And the taste. Green water, piss and semen. Afterwards, he tied the cord of his swimming trunks, double knotted. Walked away. I leant back against the rock, cool where the sun couldn't reach, and cried. Never caught his name. Because he didn't throw it. Though I called him Cliff.

How long you gonna stare out that window? Jimmy Smart says.

You—startled me, I say.

Didn't mean to. Door was open. Here, you left your wet underdrawers behind.

Sorry—

What you thinking about?

Ladybirds—

All right. Now I'm here, you mind if I have a glass of water?

Glasses are—up on the shelf.

Sweltering out there.

Here too.

I've not seen your Aunt Dreama. She all right?

She's gone to church.

Was wondering if you wanna come with me later.

Where to?

The station. Cuz I'm having a big burn up. Been hauling wood these past two days.

Might be—too warm for it, I say.

Guess it is. But it needs doing anyway, Jimmy Smart says.

Train tracks stretch into the distance, the same rusted colour as the stone station, stitching together the line between ground and sky until it's beyond blurred. The air is thick with the scent of cut wood, stirring me. Trailing behind Jimmy Smart, I have my hands pushed deep in my trouser pockets. We move past the station towards the treeline, where the indigo woodland watches us. I dislike these trees. Their branches shifting with the weight of murk and shadow. Relief comes halfway between here and there, where Jimmy Smart has hauled a big pile of wood, higher than our heads, and as wide. He's ripped down the entire fence that one time ran along the platform. The wood, once whitewashed and proud, is more grey than not after the flood. Over to the side there's three rusty oil drums in a crescent. And I feel the sting of disappointment as Petal drifts our way, wrapped in a dark lace shawl that could be a scatter of blackbirds. She is beautiful in half-light. Jimmy Smart is all big-grinned introductions. Petal reminds him she has known me most her entire life. Since we played beneath the iron bridge. Swam naked in green water. I dip my head. As though suddenly the dirt itself has said something interesting. Because me and Petal are not playmates anymore. We've hardly had two words to utter to one another since the flood. Since that night at Lynn Boxing Gym with Shane Wright and Bill Bredlau, when the storm threatened the four of us. Watching her now, curious eyes travelling the showman from dusty boots to unkempt hair, I don't hate her as I did before. Though that night swims around my head like a goldfish in a bowl, until Jimmy Smart banishes the gloom with the first flicker of fire. Rubs his palms against the backside of his trousers to clean away the muck. Petal complains about the gnats, worried they'll eat her alive. Yet the smoke from the bonfire will drive them far. For a time we sit on our drums watching the light. Every once in a while my knee knocks Jimmy Smart's. Who drinks from a bottle he passes around, made with wild things. Herbs gathered by a woman called Esme. I'm unable to fathom these plants, where they sprang from. My face feels flushed from the heat. When Petal starts humming, Jimmy Smart gets up off his drum. His eyes are full. Bright as his shirt. He shivers like something unseen has taken hold. Begins at his boots and travels upwards to his crown where his hair glows amber. The fire snaps and chucks sparks all over the place, as if he's conjured the brightness himself. He sways and hops and whirls. Petal is keeping time, the palm of her hand a steady beat against her thigh. Jimmy Smart's feet stir dust clouds, while his arms make pleasing shapes across the night, arches from here to there. Though I can't be certain where there is. Or why he'd want to cross this distance. Then Petal is on her feet moving around the fire after him. Her pretty voice haunting the night. But it's Jimmy Smart that has me mesmerised. When he dances it's like watching fire burn beneath his skin, bones for kindling. Doesn't matter that I can't see the bright blaze blistering. I just know it burns. Might be Jimmy Smart talks to the fire.

Or the drink turning his head. Alcohol is clever like that. He pulls me to my feet, where we go around and around trailing Petal. Jimmy Smart holding loosely onto my hand.

How about that fire. Was something else all right? Jimmy Smart says.

It was— I say.

Petal's something else too. Peg's worried I'll corrupt her. Like I can't stand to be around a girl without—

What?

It doesn't matter.

Does to me—

People are smallminded. I reckon it's why I'm out in black barn. Forget about it.

If you want.

I do—

Where'd you learn to—dance?

Esme taught me. Her keen on such foolish things.

I—liked it.

About before. I didn't mean anything by it, Jimmy Smart says.

Good night— I say.

I am restless. Desire is cunning like that. Can feel it in the cotton sheet beneath my back, damp from the sweltering night. My feet swing back and forth. Heels grazing floorboards sound like a rasp smoothing uneven wood. If I stretch a little further I'll be able to unsettle the pile of stones at the foot of my bed. Scatter them across the floor, where the clatter can rouse the night outside. Tell the field I'm coming. Though the noise might wake Dreama. Before, she had come home from church carrying a teacup shaped like a seashell. For near an hour she'd sat at the kitchen table, smoking her Woodbines, mesmerised by the china, so fine light from the window passed right through. Held it to her ear. Until I told her of the bonfire with Jimmy Smart. Where she wondered what sort of lunatic would light a fire in this damn heat. I'd shrugged. Reminded her he'd been hauling rotten wood for days. Dreama didn't speak another word. Least not with her mouth. Yet her face, even the way her lean fingers brushed against that pretty teacup, told me she'd seen one of her signs. Clear as anything. Same way in the black windowpane lit by lamplight, I can see myself right now. Curious how my middle is missing where the window is wedged open. How my hair, parted too neatly, is shiny as boot polish. I can still feel Jimmy Smart's warm hand on the nape of my neck, where he'd placed it after we'd quit whirling around the fire. Dizzy from spinning around and around. Him communing with the flames and all. Breathless, he'd tugged me towards him. His gaze more mysterious beneath moonlight. As though he might tip his head and howl. Instead, with a wink he glanced back at Petal, who'd stood still as the iron bridge out at the river. Then Jimmy Smart kissed me hard. I tasted cigarettes and drink and something else I don't know the name of. A puzzle. Making me hungry for more in this heat. More of him. I get up and grip the wooden window frame. The paint peeling in a pattern that reminds me of a grass snake that's shed its skin. But the window won't budge another inch. That's when I see him standing there. Jimmy Smart. Leaning against black barn in such a way as to invite me out into the hot night. He's shirtless. I'm in two minds if I should go to him, even though the field is calling. But the part of me that is neither mind has already pulled on trousers. Slipped a vest over my head. Like my skin, the cotton has held on to woodsmoke. I let my tongue travel across my dry lips. Though he's left no trace of himself there. And head outside.

Can't sleep either? Jimmy Smart says.

Not so much, I say.

Where you going?

To lie down—in the field.

You and Dreama sure are an odd pair. Coming here to this field the way you do. All times of day and night.

Might say—the same about you.

How'd you mean?

Was odd of you to—kiss me.

Told you already, it didn't mean anything. I did it to make Petal mad. She's so full of herself is all.

She'll be trouble now.

Who cares.

You not worried—she'll tell Peg?

Tell her what?

That you're—like me, I say.

I ain't, so it doesn't matter, Jimmy Smart says.

Chewing over the morning after the night before, I rub the rag along the length of the metal roller removing old ink. The wash-up solvent bites the edges of my nails where the skin is raw from scrubbing. I'm glad of this dull job. Where hands remember what to do, while thoughts shift untethered. Galloping around. After being out in the field on my back with Jimmy Smart all night, I'm worn tired. And the heat has already busted across my forehead, pooling at the edge of my ears where my hair needs cutting. Across the room Shane Wright prepares a plate. Shirt sleeves rolled all the way up. His pale arms more brawn than not. Seems his interest is elsewhere too. It strikes me sometimes Shane Wright is filled up with tragedy. There's more than muscle to him, and the square set of his jaw. Before the printshop, before I knew his name, Shane Wright's brother died in the desert. War is cruel like that. It's why he lifts heavy things. Same as the handsome men in the muscle magazines he gives me to take home. Shane Wright is training to be just like them. But really he is lifting to forget. To take his mind off the darkness. He has a big dream about going to

America. Where strong men can make more money lifting than turning printing presses. Though I don't see how. Even if they are all over the pages of *Vigour* wearing only their pleasing pouches. These distracting men who have made my dick sore with desire. Then Shane Wright comes over. Complaining about the mess I'm making. We match so in height that a plank of wood balanced on our heads would level perfectly. Though he is near twice as wide. He reminds me the rag man will be by later with Charlie. I'm to make certain the dirty cloths, sodden with ink, are bagged up. Collect the newly washed. All the while he itches his neck livid as if the air is thick with thunderflies. I nod. Knowing he is mad. Disappointed with me. His gaze now is gloomy. Without hope. As it was in the weeks after the flood, when he told me my mother wouldn't come home. That it would hurt less later to give in to the situation. And because I feel bad, I consider whether or not to stay after work. To cheer him up. Though as he yawns, throat meat coloured, I wonder if Shane Wright might not desire that after all.

You hear about church yesterday? Shane
Wright says.

Dreama—never tells me a thing 'bout church, I say.

That's understandable. Her being preoccupied with collecting the rubbish she finds along the road.
Though still, thought she'd have said something.

She hasn't.

Adie Lovekin's missing.

Disappeared?

Seems like it. No one's seen hide nor hair of her.

Know what that feels like—

Was wondering—

What might that be?

You all right to stay afterwards today?

If you want.

That's good.

Though I'm awful tired, I say.

It won't take long, Shane Wright says.

The moon is on my mind. And although it's absent from sky at dusk, as Shane Wright brings his motorcar to a standstill alongside the buckled fence, the pull is here just the same. Can feel it as surely as the heat radiating from my backside. As if Shane Wright's dick is still inside. Throbbing. His inky hands as big as shovels still holding me, instead of turning the leather steering wheel. Each time he fucks me I wonder if my underdrawers will be spoiled with blood. Him in a hurry and all. Like the first time when he broke my arsehole at fifteen years old in Lynn Boxing Gym. When I'd worried afterwards that because I talk like a girl I might be the same inside somehow. The way Dreama bleeds each month. And my mother before the flood. The three of us moved by the moon. By intuition. A tugging towards something bigger than myself. The pull to leave our field. Go someplace where people don't care if I sound like a sissy. If such a place exists. Some days I believe there's nothing but gravity that keeps me here. And I get out of Shane Wright's motorcar without saying a word. Stand still on the track while he unropes the trunk and lifts out my pushbike. Drives away. Tuck my shirt into trousers. Then go inside our house. Dreama is sat at the kitchen table smoking her Woodbine. Before her on the tabletop is a pale stone. Waxy as flint in lamplight. She tells me it came through the windowpane after I'd left first thing this morning. I nod. Slip the stone into my pocket. Later, I will place it atop the others where they're gathered in a pile at the foot of my bed. I'll patch the pane after I've fixed us something to eat. Because I worry Dreama's been sat there for the best part of the day staring out the window. The kitchen is cooler than outside. I pour us a glass each of cloudy water. Cut bread. Tomatoes from the garden. A handful of radish. Sniff yesterday's cold meat. Put out plates. It's too warm for anything hot. Besides, Dreama doesn't cook anymore. Not since the flood. When I sit down across from her at the table, she cocks her head. Peers into my eyes. I worry they've held onto before, the shape of Shane Wright naked, pounding me hard. Reflections are tricky like that. And I lower my guilty gaze. Tell her I fed Charlie the horse an apple when he came by today. But Dreama has other things on her mind. Knowing things she shouldn't.

Found the suitcase under your bed, Dreama says.

It's—nothing, I say.

Doesn't look like nothing. How long you been planning on leaving?

Since—before the flood.

Figured as much. Your mother thought it too. She tell you that?

She didn't.

Just like her to keep quiet.

I'm not leaving—now.

If you say so.

I do.

You hear about Adie Lovekin?

Shane Wright—told me.

That his motorcar I heard before?

Exact same.

He's a coward. I've seen the way he leaves you at the end of the track. First I thought he was afraid of the field. But it's not that.

You're not—making sense.

Doesn't change what I know.

And—what's that?

He put this big idea in your head. About leaving here. Going someplace else.

No—he didn't, I say.

Then who? Dreama says.

22

The missing girl fills up the townies with restlessness. Reminds me of the days after the flood. An uneasiness that was more than the sunken streets and backyards. More than doors torn from hinges and empty window frames. The people were waiting. Waiting for bodies that would surface from beneath black water, coloured blue in February light, like whales washed ashore. And now they wait to discover the whereabouts of Adie Lovekin. And with the maddening heat pushing open windows and doors across county, it's no wonder she had been taken unseen. Two days gone now, they ask themselves how they'll find her. If the tiny gold crosses will be left in her ears. Standing out back the printshop, Shane Wright tells me, between short puffs on his Woodbine, that Adie Lovekin ran away is all. No one's taken her. I suspect his pleasing mood has something to do with the ache in my backside. My own mood has haunted me all morning. A steady dread somewhere inside, hard to pin down. The same way I felt afterwards. While I waited for my own mother's body to come home. But it never did. It was then I considered leaving again. Taking the suitcase I wish Dreama had never found last night. After I'd cleared away the table and Dreama drifted outside to find a breeze, I'd gone up to my room. Lit the lamp. Pulled out the suitcase from beneath my bed. Watched it for a while. All the time a moth hammered against the glass shade. Wild in its desire. Then I unbuckled the straps, emptied clothes back into the chest of drawers. Sat back on the side of the bed. Until Dreama's hollering had me race outside. Where I'd found her alongside Jimmy Smart. The two of them behaving like lunatics. Him shirtless. His chest hairy, same colour as his head. Me wondering what his armpits might smell like. More things to think on than my head can hold. And then he'd slung his heavy arm around my shoulder, told me he had a mind to make his own cool wind. That's how we found ourselves in his motorcar. Racing through the night. Windows wound all the way down. Headlights chasing away the blackness. Everything happening at once. The showman whooping. Dreama in nothing but her shiny slip. The three of us riding across county with the wind in our hair.

On a night like tonight, when it's real warm, me
and my brother Alick would climb the big wheel.
Cuz the air's cooler up there. And quiet too, Jimmy
Smart says.

Sounds—nice, I say.

Sure was. Until Tanner would get hollering for the
two of us to get the hell down. Tanner and Alick
are twins.

They younger or—

Four years older. And they don't never let me forget it.

How'd you mean?

One time, Tanner gave me a black eye for fighting a
townie at the fair who'd called me a Pikey.

But—why'd he punish you?

That's what I'm getting at. My brothers and me,
we've rules that don't apply anywhere else. Though

I reckon, the more I think on it, that these rules are complicated.

That why—you left?

Something like that.

What 'bout the woman you talked of—Esme?

I miss her something terrible.

She tell you—you'd come here?

You'd best go inside. Your Dreama'll wonder what we're doing out here, Jimmy Smart says.

Guess so, I say.

By mid-day the dread inside has drifted away. Gone across the distance where it's settled on Shane Wright's shoulders. For the past hour he's been complaining about the Heidelberg. The steady pounding wearing on his nerves, until he's cradling his head in defeat. Even though every window is hooked open the rollers are scumming-up in the dry air. I pull a single sheet from the stack at the end of the printing press. The ink smells lively. Smudged around the edge of the paper, as if the letters themselves are tiny volcanoes erupting ash everywhere. The water is evaporating too fast in the heat. Shane Wright knows this already. And more. He tells me something's broken. That maybe the fountain has turned bad. That's when I tell him about last night's big breeze. How we could use Jimmy Smart here now. Shane Wright's gaze becomes baffled. Until I explain the three of us riding around the fields, thundering past Coalyard Creek with the windows wound down. I don't mention we were shirtless. That Dreama was wearing just her silk slip shimmering in the air. Because he wouldn't want to hear it. Jimmy Smart has gotten beneath his skin in the same way a troublesome splinter might. If it weren't for the field Shane Wright would have driven over before now. To take a good look at the showman living out in black barn. But he won't go near the field. Curses are powerful like that. And then he wipes his forehead with a rag. Lifts off the fountain bottle and hurls it across the room. I head outside for my break. Here in the yard I can hear Mac Sam take a long piss on account of all the water he's been guzzling. Afterwards, he wants to know what the banging's all about. I tell him he should go see for himself. Sit down on the floor in a piece of shadow and lean against the wall. Beside my head is the surprising purple flower I've seen before. Living there in the old mortar. Makes me wonder what another job might look like. In a different place. Where I've no need to scrub ink from my nails each day. Or have concern my shirt will be spoiled because it's too hot to wear overalls. Then I open-up my lunch tin, leave the sandwich inside. Take out my notebook and pencil, turn to a clean page, and carefully write the name Adie Lovekin. Underlined.

What you writing down this time? Shane Wright says.

Nothing—much, I say.

But something—

'Bout the missing girl.

What about Adie Lovekin?

Dunno—just yet.

You're always scribbling something in that bloody book. How come you never let me read any of it?

Didn't know—it bothered you.

Some days, it does.

My break's—over.

I'm sorry about before. It's the damn heat wearing on my nerves.

If you say so.

I do. Mac Sam says we can have tomorrow off.

How come?

Reckons he'll have to drive across county for the new part we'll need.

Uh huh.

What'd you suppose you'll do all day? Shane Wright says.

I'll think of—something, I say.

Wolferton platform is abandoned. The train somewhere between here and Hunstanton, moving weary townies along twisted train tracks to cool off in green sea water. Where they'll hunger after iced cream and sand. I haven't seen the sea since before the flood. After my mother was carried away. Taken to the bottom of the Wash, tangled amongst lost nets and trawler rigging. Nothing left for me and Dreama to bury in dirt. A place to come to with flowers when we ache. But I've not come to this place to think about how clever water can be. And I lean my pushbike against the rusted red wall. Wipe sweaty palms on the back of my trousers. If Mac Sam hadn't been on his way across county to pick up a part for the press I'd be restless in the printshop yard instead of here. Restless because Jimmy Smart has been absent these past two days. No sign of him out in black barn. His motorcar gone. With no one around, I head around back. From here the empty oil drums look like cattle, broken off from the heard grazing in the charred grass where the bonfire had been. My left hand tingles with the thought of Jimmy Smart hurling us around the flames, holding on to me. His amber hair oily. Face that needed to be shaved. Then his kiss that didn't mean anything except to make Petal wild. And wild she'd been. Her gaze that made me wonder if Jimmy Smart sees me more like a girl than not. With no way around it, I walk back, for what I came here to find out. Inside the station, beneath the clock, Petal sweeps the floor. She's red from the effort. Her hair darker than it really is, tied-up in a knot. She looks over but doesn't speak. I lean against the wall with my arms folded. Waiting. The only sound is the brush rushing across the stone floor. After a while she tells me I have a big nerve coming here showing my face. Unwelcome, I shrug. Hope that my hurt doesn't flush across my skin. How she can still do this is a mystery to me. Then she disappears through a brick arch. I follow her outside. Mad, Petal turns around too fast and I bump into her. Her breath smells of chicory, same as the dandelions harassing their field. Behind, there's an old wooden station sign from before. Paint peeling in the heat, red and blue giving way to a surprising shade of green no one can remember. Because I can't look at Petal, I think about the wood. That if I pushed my ear against the grain, might I hear wind rushing through leaves. Same way the sea makes waves inside a shell.

You won't find him here. That's who you're looking for—Jimmy Smart? Petal says.

It—is, I say.

He's gone back to the showpeople.

The fair—

That's what I said.

For—how long?

How should I know?

Something—bad happen?

You'll have to ask him.

I will.

You know—

What?

He's not like Shane Wright. What you both are.

And—what am I?

You gonna make me say it?

29

If it makes you—feel better.

It doesn't.

Just so—you know. Nothing's going on with Jimmy Smart, I say.

Could've fooled me, Petal says.

Jimmy Smart's old man was a boxer. Everyone called him Bullet. Making a big bang moving up and down the country from fair to fair, pocketing more money from boxing booths than he'd seen turning the gallopers. One time he won a fight against a welterweight called Micky Joe, and earned himself two grown lions that went by the names Ezzah and Afreen. But Bullet knew nothing about keeping wild animals. Jimmy Smart's eyes grow dark when he talks about those lions. As if there's a storm between his ears and nowhere else. I lean in a little closer. Wanting more. To hear them growl inside his head at the passers-by. Not knowing nothing of his world. Where travelling fairs are conjured in morning light only to disappear soon after. Tales of families woven tight as rope, hitched to the past. Before, I'd left Petal glum-faced at Wolferton station, and rode my pushbike home to find Jimmy Smart's shiny motorcar filling up my eyes. Behind that the field, more gilt than green. This place like no other anywhere. And the restlessness had eased away. When I'd walked through the backdoor I found the showman sat across from Dreama at our kitchen table. A conspiring gaze about them both. I said nothing at all. Poured myself a glass of cloudy water. Guzzled it down. All the while Dreama smoked her Woodbine watching the showman. Might be she is taken with him. That she knows something of my own desire. Until Jimmy Smart had suggested we go out to black barn. To talk some. And that's how I find myself sat on the fold-out bed beside a wooden crate. Atop a worn leather wetpack, his bottle of flavoured alcohol, and a photograph of him with a black woman. He hands me the picture of Esme. Tells me she's been sick with a terrible fever he worried wouldn't break. Her delirious with tales of him being sixteen years old and Bullet all but beating him to death over those two lions. I shake my head in disbelief. Because I know what Jimmy Smart is fixing to tell me. And now, with the heat and smells making me dizzy, I've no ear for it.

My old man was a stubborn sonofabitch, Jimmy Smart says.

Never—knew mine, I say.

Maybe it's better that way. I sure hated my old man.

Because he beat you?

And the rest. There ain't enough time on this earth for me to go over all the reasons.

All right. But—

Go on—

What happened to—never mind.

Ezzah and Afreen? You won't like it. He killed 'em. Day after I turned sixteen, and beat me blue.

Why'd he do it?

Cuz he could.

I don't—understand.

Some things just are. Doesn't matter that you might want it to be otherwise. Or how hard you try to make it right. I guess—

What?

He didn't like the way I cared for them lions. Or maybe, how fond they were of me.

I'm—sorry.

I'd lie on the roof of their cage, thinking about their predicament. Nobody knew them better than me. I'd listen to them. Pacing back and forth. Hear the hurt inside. Inside myself as well. Until we were more alike than not— Jimmy Smart says.

Roaring with lions— I say.

Dreama is a tar-black silhouette in the doorframe that Jimmy Smart had left open to let the heat out. Interrupting him telling me more about his old man, who wanted to be welterweight champion of the world. I hadn't noticed how long we'd been out here, while Dreama had fixed dinner. I wonder if she is less untethered with the showman living in black barn. Even the shape of her appears different today. Surprising me how pretty angles can be. Since the flood she's been absent from my world. Unable to care about everyday chores. Leaving me to fix our evening meal. Scrub clothes against the wooden washboard on Sunday while she goes to church. Mend socks and patch broken windowpanes. I ache for how she was before the flood. Her and my mother. Before dark water raced around our field turning the surrounding dirt barren with salt. She tells us again there's food waiting and walks away. Taking the pleasing shape with her. Jimmy Smart hops up off the fold-out bed. Stretches. Seems to me, like Bullet, he has a boxer's build. Doubt I am a similar shape to my old man. Then he collects the glass bottle from atop the wooden crate and heads for the house. Me trailing behind. A sudden irritation that I'll have to share him with Dreama. Inside, she has laid out the table with mismatched china. Before me a bluish-white plate with a scatter of rubbed violets around the rim. Jimmy Smart has a willow pattern. And Dreama's plate, pale green and oval-shaped. Some of this china belongs to other people's lives. Carried across fields during the flood. Left unbroken. Collected by Dreama from alongside the road on her way to pray. Wandering into ruined fields unguarded by scarecrows, where God has gifted her something whole. God is mysterious like that. Though she doesn't say grace. Instead, tells us to help ourselves to sawn chunks of heavy bread. Tomatoes and onions from our garden. Cold potatoes leftover from yesterday, sliced and seasoned. Jimmy Smart pours each of us a measure from his bottle. Tells Dreama the wild things Esme uses to flavour the alcohol. Elderflower, basil, mint and rosemary. She puts down her Woodbine long enough to chuck back the liquid. Coughs madly. Before raising her glass to the three of us. I wish she would steady on. More so when the showman pours another. Winks at me. Assures us these tomatoes are the sweetest he's yet tasted. It's because of the soil. But I don't proclaim it out loud. Might be the curse would come up. And he's rising from his chair. Gone outside to use the lean-to. Dreama's gaze is puzzling. Her eyes another kind of blue I've no name for. Hair more yellow than golden. She smokes her Woodbine. A small pool of sweat has gathered in-between her collarbone, threatening to run over.

Showmen are different, Dreama says.

Different—how? I say.

Unlike other men. Way they see things. Comes from them living the way they do.

Is that so—

I like him. The field does too.

Doubt the dirt cares either way.

You know everything now?

No.

And don't look at me like that. I'm not crazy.

Never said as much—

Besides, you're keen on him. Can see it plain as anything.

Dunno—what you mean.

You're fooling yourself. Way you always do.

Doesn't—concern you.

Does when he's pissing fifteen feet from here,
Dreama says.

Least twenty, I say.

In my nightmare blackbirds smothered Adie Lovekin.
Though the feathers didn't belong to birds themselves.
Instead, printed on tiny pieces of paper, torn-edged and
pasted all over her small body. Even the soles of her feet.
Blinking can't remove the remnant, disturbing the inside
of my eyelids. I am damp with sweat. Naked. The cotton
sheet kicked off the bed, threatening to tip my pile of stones.
I get up. Walk the floor to the china basin that sits atop the
chest-of-drawers. Splash my face with tepid water. But it
doesn't help any. Or stifle the groan, more of a growl, escap-
ing my throat. My head hurts something awful. Hurts from
recalling the evening before with Dreama and Jimmy Smart.
Three of us drinking his fresh bottle of alcohol. Full with
wild things he'd brought back after returning from Esme's
sickbed. And when the light had turned from a dim glow
to dark, Dreama lit lamps. Their cloudy glass shades casting
pleasing pools of brightness. Cigarette smoke everywhere.
The showman talking big about all the places he'd seen.
Here and overseas. How in each one the townies are all the
same. Ignorant. Dreama agreeing. Her glass turning on the
tabletop while she waited for him to fill it. Telling us she
hadn't been hardly anywhere since before the war. Then in
a darker tone, that I had a mind to move to another town on
account of the suitcase she'd found beneath my bed. Hearing
this Jimmy Smart had laid his heavy hand on my shoulder

and kneaded the muscle there. Drink turning his gaze black until no colour remained. Protesting town wouldn't do me any good. Because I'm different. Me now wondering if he meant my sissy-sounding voice, or something else. Either way I'll find no answer with this distraction, my need to urinate badly. I pull on underdrawers and vest. Leave my boots at the backdoor. The dirt is warm and pleasing beneath the soles of my feet. Then I'm tugging open the door of the lean-to where Jimmy Smart is mid-piss. I'm desperate. He shuffles over one foot. And I take out my dick and piss alongside him. I'd whistle if I knew how to. Instead I stare straight ahead at the back boards. There's a knot in the wood eyeballing me. On his way out, Jimmy Smart wants to know if I'd like a ride to the printshop today. I agree quietly, finding it especially hard to speak while pissing. He tells me to hurry up. I return to my bedroom. Finish dressing. And go back outside. Inside his motorcar I wind down the window all the way. The breeze is cool against my neck. Hair still damp from before. I glance at Jimmy Smart. He needs a shave. Hair oily. Though he doesn't seem like his head hurts in the same way mine does. Driving along these roads like the law are behind him. Either side us the fields are nothing but dead dirt. Green gone away. And the showman wants to know why we don't plant the field. Or rent it out. That me and Dreama could use the money. That we're being foolish.

Out with it, Jimmy Smart says.

It's—nothing, I say.

This about me calling you foolish?

36

No—

The curse then?

It's not—straightforward.

Nothing ever is.

I had a nightmare—is all.

Tell me.

'Bout—Adie Lovekin.

She that missing girl?

Exact same. She was—covered in birds.

What kind of birds?

Blackbirds.

You gonna write that down in that notebook of yours? Cuz I've seen you. Scribbling all the time. What exactly you writing about?

Mostly—what people say.

You ever write down my words? Jimmy Smart says.

The ones I care for, I say.

Mac Sam is waiting for me inside the printshop. Ringing a rag between his hands, making me wonder if he wishes it were my neck. Absently, I tug at my shirt collar, where my hair needs cutting. The heat hangs here, spreading out across my shoulders. The air around us, yesterday's and

37

stale, makes my headache worsen. I dip my head and apologise. Though I don't understand his concern because the Heidelberg is still. Inkless. The rollers removed, sat on the workbench. The metal side hung open. I suppose waiting for the part that'll make everything turn again. I believe Mac Sam hates me. In the same way he might a stray dog shitting in the yard. Outside, I find Shane Wright smoking his Woodbine. Smoke purple in morning light. By his feet is a tin bucket of turpentine. I peer in. Like a coiled snake the chain from the printing press in soaking in solvent. Shedding ink in the liquid. The smell makes my nostrils itch. My head spins some. He asks why I'm late. I shrug. Then he wants to know if I've heard about Adie Lovekin. My stomach whirls and flutters madly. Shane Wright tells me, between short drags on his cigarette, that the missing girl is no longer lost. Instead, found stumbling the evening before by two townies out at Nar Shed, past the Muckworks, south of Lynn. I begin breathing again. And he goes on to tell me it was two boys that came upon her. Blindfolded and her hands still tied. Them boys chasing trouble out there beneath the hundred-foot high shed. Bombed in forty-four, it looms in the wasteland. A rusted skeleton pushing itself from concrete into clouds. After the flood washed fertilizer from the Muckworks into the ground, where it gathered in deep wells around the place, the townies tell their children to keep away. And now because of the turpentine and little pieces of paper printed with feathers flickering behind my eyelids, I throw up alongside the bucket. Splashing Shane Wright's black boots. He tells me I belong in bed. Until whatever is addling me is no more. Promises to fix it with Mac Sam. I nod. Tell him I'll have to walk the distance on account of Jimmy Smart giving me a ride here in his motorcar before. His gaze becomes narrow. So small I'd never

know the hazel colour of his eyes if I hadn't worked with
him these past four years. Shane Wright is jealous. Wants
to drive me home himself. But I have no mind to return to
the field. Or Dreama. I push past him. Feels like I'm fifteen
years old again. When he took me to Lynn Boxing Gym.
Him holding on to me with his inky hands he'd not cared to
clean. Promising he'd go slowly. While I'm left wondering
how much say I have in what he wants. Because desire can
be cunning. Then afterwards, the ache in my backside trou-
bling me. Blood too. Discovering the places his hands had
been by the ink he left behind. A black smudge on my left
shoulder. Another beside my bellybutton. Thigh. Beneath
my balls. A map of sorts.

I'll not have you walk home, Shane Wright says.

Doesn't—concern you, I say.

Does when you're coming to work hungover.

I'm not—

Could've fooled me. Your bloody showman's
no good.

Don't see—what Jimmy Smart has to do with it.

You're not yourself. Since he's been out in
black barn.

Then who am I?

Beats me. You know what I reckon? There's
something going on. Between the two of you.

39

There's nothing—

You with this Jimmy Smart fella now?

It's not like that.

What is it like, then?

Dunno—

Sure you do.

I like him—is all.

He know about me?

A little bit.

Must think me an idiot. Or worse.

He doesn't think—nothing like that.

This us over then? Shane Wright says.

Not as far as I know, I say.

Lynn station is stiller than it ought to be. Sweaty children too hot to run around have their backsides on wooden benches. Heavy heads lolled sideways, unable to make trouble. Mothers fan themselves with pale hands. Two porters carry luggage like they're hauling rocks in a quarry. And there's steam every-where. All along the platform. Twirling around legs, sliding beneath the soles of shoes that tread soot into the stone floor. Beside me a redheaded man in a striped white shirt puts down his brown suitcase, seesaws his shoulders. He smells the same as Jimmy Smart's bonfire. Reminding me of that night. What

40

I have to do. Why I'm pushing my hand into my pocket and handing over coins at the glass window. In return for a single ticket to Wolferton. Once there I intend to ask Jimmy Smart about the things I'm thinking. His kiss that meant nothing more than making Petal jealous. Because I don't believe it. And the lean-to this morning. Pissing alongside one another. Then back further to his underwear soaked clear, when the moon had tried to fool me shimmering in a bucket of water. Though I haven't decided exactly which question I'll begin with. Or when it comes down to it, if I'll be able to speak at all. My sissy mouth getting in the way of everything inside. All at once the whistle's piping, and I get on board the third-class carriage, behind the man in the striped shirt. He's taller than I first thought. I sit down on the leather bench across from him. Steam clears from the window while I watch the town fall behind. Past the redbrick chimney. Muckworks. Nar Shed where Shane Wright told me two boys found Adie Lovekin blindfolded. I close my eyes. Unsure what I'll see inside the lids. Blackbirds. The moon bright as a dinnerplate. Stacked stones. Dreama turning. A yellowed sky above black water. Blue china. My mother standing moodily wearing her green dress. The showman laying alongside me in the field, chewing a piece of grass. I snap them back open. Thing about Jimmy Smart, I believe, is that he encourages me to dream in a way I wouldn't ordinarily. And when the redheaded man wants to know if I'm traveling to the shore, I shake my head. Tell him not this day.

What you doing here, cuz you're the last person I was expecting to see, Jimmy Smart says.

41

I'm—sick, I say.

What's wrong with ya?

Just a—headache is all.

But, it's more than that?

Dunno—where to start.

Beginning's as good a place as any.

People reckon—at first I'm deaf. Or mute.
Sometimes both.

Idiots. Go on.

Then when I talk—they know everything at once.
Least—they believe they do.

How'd you mean?

Me—sounding like a sissy.

You shouldn't care.

But—it's the truth. I'm what they say—I am.

I know that.

Don't it bother you? I say.

It's more agreeable than not, Jimmy Smart says.

Jimmy Smart quits when I pull back some. His fingers no longer pushed against my middle, north of my bellybutton, stirring everything up. He just shrugs. Adjusts the tilt of his porter's cap a little. Tells me he's work still to do. That there'll be time to talk afterwards, when his shift's over. Then he leans in, and I brace myself for this confidence. The showman's breath warm against my cheek, then disturbing my earhole, as unhurriedly he suggests I adjust my trousers. Being around him interferes with everything, like the hairs on my arm during a thunderstorm. While he walks away in a gust of steam, I take care of the situation happening in my underdrawers. Knowing bashfulness has turned my face redder than the bricks behind me. Sometimes, I believe my dick can be a misery. Causing more misfortune than not. As it had the night of the storm. When Petal and Bill Bredlau found me and Shane Wright together at Lynn Boxing Gym. And though I came here to tell Jimmy Smart these things he's conjured inside of me, it's hard to forget where I'm standing. In Peg's home. I've no desire to run into Petal. Her eternally mad at me. Making me miserable. Dreama reckons misery comes more easily to some people than others. And with my crotch decent, and the platform all but empty, I watch the train disappear on its way to the shore. Wander around the station side. Where I put my backside down on the bottom step of the stairs leading up to the white-washed signal box. The wood warm and sprung. Smoke a Woodbine. A big shiny bluebottle flies around my head. I swat it away. But it's back bothering me, along with my busy head. That still aches from the bucket of turpentine, and the night drinking alongside Dreama and Jimmy Smart. Perhaps more too. Standing on the platform before with Jimmy Smart. Steam everywhere. Him telling me I'm more agreeable than not. Even with my sissy mouth getting in the way of everything. I want to know how I'm more agreeable. Then Peg is hollering behind me, coming down the wooden steps from the signal box like a whirlwind.

43

Taking hold of me as if I were kin. Until it's hard to breathe. Wanting to know why the hell she's not laid eyes on me since the showman moved into black barn. I shrug. Is Dreama sick she demands. I shake my head hurriedly. Tell her everything is just fine. That I came to talk to Jimmy Smart. That's when she sighs. Tips her head sideways and wants to know all about the situation with me and Petal.

You and my Petal ever gonna sort out this thing between you? God knows what's going on. Because she won't tell me one word of it, Peg says.

Dunno—that there's anything to sort out, I say.

You playing with me?

I ain't.

Should bang your heads together. Might make you see sense.

I guess.

You know, eventually I'll find out. Sooner than later. Seems to me Jimmy Smart's not helping any.

How'd you mean?

Him and my Petal don't exactly see eye to eye.

That so?

I reckon. What about your Dreama? How in the hell is she? Expect it's some help having Jimmy Smart living out in black barn.

44

Some—

She still out in that goddamn field night and day? I just can't make sense of it myself. Though I know she's not been right since that night.

He's good—with Dreama.

And you?

Huh?

He good to you.

He is—

And those windowpanes. He mend them yet?

Not yet.

You see that he does, Peg says.

I will, I say.

Dirt can be hard as stone to get beneath. Determined to pull my weight I take over from Jimmy Smart. Who puts his back against the wall. Sighs. His cap turned around to keep the moisture from hounding his forehead. Leans in such a way that his shadow appears as another man laid at his boots. Who died without any commotion. We're round back behind the redbrick station. Disturbing a patch of unbroken ground with a pickaxe that might be older than both our years combined. Wood smooth. Steel no longer silvered, instead a pleasing shade of brown. Each time I strike the dirt a cloud appears, then disappears. Pieces of shiny flint scatter. And I grunt with the effort. He tells me to quit arguing with the ground. Lights two cigarettes. Passes me the spare. We stand side by side and smoke our Woodbines in the afternoon heat. Further down our shirts are hung on a bent nail. This pleases me. Because for the past hours I've watched him wield the pickaxe. While I followed behind with my shovel. Mesmerised. Muscles yawning beneath his skin, polished with sweat. This hole we're digging is on account of the new pipe Peg wants laying in. Though I don't rightly know why. Across the way two blackbirds hop back and forth. Beady black eyes keen on us. Jimmy Smart tells me they're after the worms is all. But Dreama would believe otherwise. Certain they mean something more. After my dream of Adie Lovekin smothered in feathers I'm inclined to agree. I pick up a stone and hurl it at them. They fly away. Then Jimmy Smart reminds me this hole won't dig itself. Collects the pickaxe from where I'd laid it to rest. Swings it onto his shoulder. Reckons afterwards, when his shift is over, we can ride out to the iron bridge to cool off before returning home to the field. My ears are pleased to hear this. Right now I'd welcome the river. To leap beneath a big moon, like we did that night. And I've been wondering when we'd get to talk. Alone. That's when from behind Petal tells the two of us that a swim sounds like a fine idea. We turn around together. She stands waiting, fanning herself with her hand. Her pretty pale-blue dress the same colour as her eyes. Mouth a little ajar. The showman sighs. Though it's hard to hear. Behind, the blackbirds have retuned, pecking dirt. Jimmy Smart confesses the swim is more a chance to get cleaned up before dinner, than anything else. Petal doesn't speak. Instead, her gaze goes from me to the showman, and travels back again. I fold my arms across my bare chest. Seems she's hellbent on proving something to somebody. Though it won't be easy because some things are difficult to prove. After a moment, she turns

and disappears down the side of the station, leaving us silent.
But for the blackbirds squawking. Jimmy Smart lowers the
pickaxe. Sets back to work. Hammering the dirt. Again and
again. Like a madman. Until he's kicked up a cloud of amber
dust that whirls around us. Me supposing by sundown he'll
be left with a palmful of blisters.

Cuz Petal knows I'm not interested in that way.
But she won't let it be. And no good'll come of it,
Jimmy Smart says.

Guess—not, I say.

You wanna tell me what went on between the two of you?

Nothing much to tell.

It's all right if you don't want to. None of my
business after all. But you don't have to lie.

Shane Wright—

What about him?

He found himself—in the same situation.

You mean Petal was keen on him too?

Since I've known her—Petal's chased after
everything she can't have. Then—

Go on.

Night of the storm—she found me and Shane
Wright together at Lynn Boxing Gym.

How'd you mean?

Shane Wright is—like me.

Can imagine Petal being none too pleased finding that out. The hard way.

'Bout as bad as it could be. Bill Bredlau giving us away. Two of us—naked and all.

Why'd he do that?

Dunno—

Does Peg know? Or your Dreama?

Dreama sees everything.

She does at that.

Everything—changed that night.

You're not wrong. Though you know what I'm wondering? Petal being the way she is. How come she's not told the whole damn town? Jimmy Smart says.

Reckon Bill Bredlau's as good as reason as any— I say.

Wild with hoppers, we're on the riverbank. Me and Jimmy Smart. Our eyes hungry for the wet waiting before us. Untying leather bootlaces, tugging shirts over heads. Unbuckling belts, pulling off trousers. Until we're naked, and the showman has a block of cream-coloured soap in his palm. Taken from the station toilet after his shift, that he proposes we take turns with. Before, in his motorcar on the road here, past fields where crops don't care to grow any longer, he tells me how the pleasing lemon scent reminds him of the wood-soap he uses to clean the gallopers. That the painted horses get as dirty as skin from all the steam and turning and townies who ride them. Then how surprising paint can be. All the colours laid down by Italians before the war. Who charmed the colour with whispered words, until thirty horses kick and snort and hurtle around. All but a single grey horse unlike the others. Me wanting to know why, and Jimmy Smart shrugging. Because he's back to his rules again that don't apply anywhere else. And I wonder if I am more alike this horse than not. Without colour. My sissy mouth getting in the way. Now the showman is splashing into green water. Calling me to follow. With the wet shimmering around our legs, I wait while he washes himself first with the soap. Rubbing the pale block against his hairy chest. Armpits. Across his shoulders. Then lower. Until he's handing me the soap, and I can clean the dirt and heat from my own skin. I wash quickly while he rinses himself off. When Jimmy Smart comes up from beneath the wet, skin polished, he wants to know if I'll wash his hair. Puts his back to me. I work suds into the tangled mess. Throw the block behind us onto the riverbank. Scrub his hair clean. Coils catching between my fingers, while he makes small noises that stir me. I'm afraid to move. In case my dick pushes against his backside. All at once my hands hang in the air as Jimmy Smart disappears beneath. When he surfaces, he has turned around. His gaze unbashful. A dare. Darker than I have ever known it. We take hold of each other's dicks. Lean in. Our bodies damp. Hearts pounding. Faces pressed together. I close my eyes. Soak up what's happening. While we work on each other. For a time all I can hear are hands beating, flies buzzing, the river running. Jimmy Smart comes first, splashing me. The sudden slickness surprising. Tipping me over the edge, like falling, until my own semen shoots across his belly. And a small whining noise escapes my mouth. I move my mouth closer to his. But Jimmy Smart drops back into the river. Making a splash.

You know what I reckon? Jimmy Smart says.

Dunno, I say.

Should have told Petal before, that she could come with us swimming.

But—

What?

Nothing—

Might be it's time the two of you put things right.

Dunno—that I care to.

That might be. Though I reckon if you don't, before much longer everyone will find out about you and Shane Wright.

Not sure—I care.

You should. Dare say he'd have something to say as well.

Why'd you—care?

Just cuz.

Sometimes—

What?

I wish I'd never—been with him that night.

I know what you're thinking. And you'd be wrong. You should forget about it. There's no use tormenting yourself. It won't do any good. No one saw what was coming that night, Jimmy Smart says.

Might be—Dreama did, I say.

Shaking the river from his hair, Jimmy Smart tells me I might be surprised to know fortune-tellers aren't all that common. That if Dreama does have a gift she's likely unused to it. Wades out of the green water, onto the bank, where he collects his underdrawers and wipes himself down. Pulls up trousers past his pale backside. Lights a Woodbine. Suddenly I feel foolish. Understanding my sissy ways are agreeable until Jimmy Smart has emptied his balls. His manner reminding me we're unalike. That he's not the same. I chew on my bottom lip. Glad my dick has settled down. Climb out of the wet onto the riverbank, and dry myself off. Jimmy Smart pats the grass beside him. I sit down. Light a Woodbine of my own. The smoke rough in the back of my throat. In between us is the pleasing-smelling soap. Dry grass stuck to the surface. Maybe even some of the showman's amber-coloured hair. Above, the iron bridge casts a clever shadow that's cool to be beneath. In the distance I can hear a freight train. Carrying sand somewhere no doubt. Maybe two miles out. Then Jimmy Smart starts talking about Petal again. How pretty she was in her blue dress. I want to remind him how hard he'd hammered the dirt with the pickaxe in the hours beforehand. How no good could come from her interest in him. Though I keep quiet. And smoke some more. Because the whole time Jimmy Smart talks I can see where our being here is heading. Him wanting to prove he's something other than what he is. When what I want is to be in black barn. Laid out together. Two of us still unclothed. Tracing trails with our fingertips on damp skin. Disappearing into otherness. But we're not in black barn. And by the look of things the showman is near to sleep. His eyes closed. Back against the bank. I watch him for a while. Until I'm sure he's out. Take the block of soap and tuck it into my pocket. On the road, past his motorcar shimmering there, I consider the showman's lone galloper. Different from all the others. Turning again and again but never getting anywhere. Seems to me I am that horse, hellbent on chasing these things I desire. Dangerous things that cause me more misfortune than not. Might be Jimmy Smart is the most dangerous yet.

You finished messing around? Cuz I'm done being ignored now? Jimmy Smart says.

Go—away, I say.

That'd be right. Back like before when I first moved into black barn. You swallowing everything down. This ain't easy for me.

It doesn't matter—

Don't know why it's hard for you to understand.

52

Huh?

My whole entire life people have been
disappointing me.

How'd—I disappoint you?

By clearing off like you did. Leaving me asleep on
the riverbank. Cuz it wasn't enough. What we did.
I'm right, ain't I?

I thought—

What? Go on.

That we're the same somehow.

I told you already. I ain't that way.

You can't—even say it.

What's it matter?

Just does. What 'bout where words come from?

Suppose I was just running off at the mouth is all,
Jimmy Smart says.

You're wrong. And—I don't reckon people have
been disappointing you your whole entire life. It's—
the other way around, I say.

Dreama is somewhere else. Untethered. Even though she's
sat at the pine table in our kitchen across from me. Between
us a small wooden box with the discarded lid laid alongside.
I know she will have found this abandoned by the flood

alongside a field on her walk home from church. I take hold of the box. The wood is pale and soft and warm. As though sap runs through its heart. I turn it over. Pasted on the underside is a faded piece of paper. *Libraire Au Nain Bleu. Arts Divinatoires. Le Pendule Paradiamagnétique.* Beneath, an address. *38, Av. De la Victoire, France.* My gaze returns to Dreama's hand. Her holding a narrow piece of frayed red silk, where beneath a pendulum swings madly around and around. Her own gaze mesmerised by the cut-glass ball turning. Alive with light. All the while muttering something my ears are unable to follow, same as the writing on the box. Apprehension fills me. And what Dreama might do with such an object. Where it might move her. As if things weren't bad enough already. I imagine this box before the war. The child who'd held it on the other side of the Wash. Before a soldier had tucked the toy into his khaki knapsack, and carried it home to lay before his own child. Who that child might have been. And where it lay the night of the flood. When water rushed across the county displacing everything. Except our field. If things were different between me and Jimmy Smart I'd ask him what I should do about Dreama and her pendulum. Him having knowledge of fortune-tellers and the like. But I've not laid eyes on him since my bedroom, after the riverbank. He'd appeared at the door as if he'd climbed a hill mad with wind, instead of our stairs. And we'd argued. Him accusing me of something I didn't know I'd done. And now this here predicament with Dreama.

I know what you're thinking, Dreama says.

What's that? I say.

No good can come from fooling with such a thing.

That pendulum—tell you that?

Might be I found it for a reason.

Doubt it. Just the—flood is all. Same as the china washed up.

I feel like before that night again.

You're just restless.

This really about me and my pendulum?

How'd you mean?

Seems to me, you're mad with something else.

Huh?

Heard the two of you before. Arguing—

You were eavesdropping?

It's still my house.

You're right—

Two of you at each other. I don't care for it.

Me neither.

What do you think Jimmy Smart would say about this here pendulum?

He'd tell you—it wouldn't have made any difference.

Might be his Esme would believe otherwise.

Don't reckon so.

That night. If I'd known— Dreama says.

Doubt even God knew 'bout it, I say.

Unable to stand watching Dreama a moment longer, I go outside. Past black barn. To the edge of our field. Stand where green bends towards the horizon. Sometimes Dreama's so similar to my mother it hurts to look at her. And now even the grass here reminds me of her. Startling the way this colour is the same as my mother's pretty dress that day. Before it disappeared beneath her heavy wool coat in winter. Standing beneath a sky wild with weather, morning of the flood. I close my eyes. Reminded of my small mistake. And how it had maddened her. When she'd taken the padlock from her pocket and held it in the palm of her hand. Where the metal had looked alive and oily in the strange yellow light. As if it were a blackbird curled beneath its wing. As though any moment it might unfold and soar someplace else. I'd wanted to be that bird. Instead, without a word, I'd turned around towards black barn. The planks groaned with a sudden wind, testing the iron nails. Some days I'd hated black barn more than the townies who called me a sissy. The same men who were once the boys that hurled stones at me on the walk home from school. Then with no way around it, I'd walked the distance to the door. Fastened the padlock in place to make right my wrong. When I turned back my mother was already riding away on her pushbike. Me not knowing I'd never gaze on her again. Now standing here, I've a mind to go look for the padlock. Tell Jimmy Smart he can find another black barn, with another fold-out bed to put his back against. Though I'm not sure I mean it. Because anger is bewildering like that. Part of me wants to lay down unseen beneath Jimmy Smart. In the cool dirt there. Beneath the hatch his fold-out bed rests upon. Listen to him sleep. In the weeks after the flood, when Dreama wouldn't talk to no one, I'd cleared out everything hidden beneath the hatch. Until there was room enough to bury a horse if I'd had such a beast to bury. And the townies stopped coming out to our field at nightfall. Like they had during the war. When aeroplanes hummed overhead. All at once I am not alone. Jimmy Smart is standing alongside me. He smells like his bottle of herbs soaked in alcohol. I dare not hardly glance his way. While I wait without a word.

You and Dreama and this field baffle me. Three of you make as much sense as me and my brothers. And that's saying something, Jimmy Smart says.

Don't see what's so—confusing, I say.

That's because you're blind to it.

How'd you mean?

Not one of you are easy to understand. This goddamn curse. Your peculiar ways. Dreama out there turning in the field.

Leave Dreama—out of this.

What about you? Should I leave you be, also?

If—that's what you want.

It is.

Because—I'm a sissy?

Cuz you're behaving like a child.

I'm not what you think I am.

Then what are you?

Forget 'bout it.

I won't.

All right. I'm—no coward.

You saying I am?

Reckon so— I say.

I ought to smack you one for calling me that.
Keep clear of me Eli. I'll not tell you twice, Jimmy
Smart says.

The man who took Adie Lovekin has kept her voice.
Returned her with a tongue unable to utter his name. I
know this because over dinner Dreama tells me so. How
the Reverend spoke to his congregation. That Jesus will
cure her muteness in time. But even Dreama doesn't believe
his lie. Tells me she doubts the girl will utter a word again.
Lights her Woodbine. Brushes her lip to rid the small piece
of cigarette paper hanging there. In half-light her wide eyes
are more black than blue with an aversion for the Reverend.
I sigh even though I don't mean to. Wondering why she
bothers going to church to begin with. Unable to fathom

God myself. Because of the flood. For taking my mother. And before that. The way he sees fit to make one man one way and me another. With my sissy mouth. What Dreama tells me are my soft ways. Along with clean fingernails and keeping my hair smooth and combed down. These things I believe give everything away at once. Agitated, I put my back to Dreama who murmurs misgivings about the Reverend and Adie Lovekin. Concentrate on stacking dinnerplates on the shelf, where they rattle a small warning. One day the whole shelf will come crashing down, and the kitchen floor will be coloured with shards of pretty patterns from the peculiar china Dreama has collected after the flood. Or the women who washed them before will come looking for them. From the window here I can see black barn hunkered down. And my stomach takes to turning. My head too. Jimmy Smart's warning wedged in the back of my throat. I'm unable to swallow it. Two times since before, I've considered walking the dirt between here and there to apologise. Try to take back calling him a coward. Even though I wasn't entirely wrong. Truth can be tricky like that. Might be this word though is unmoveable. Like a rock in the field. But I want to get beneath him. To what stays hidden. Even if it does cause me more misfortune than not. Then, as if I've conjured him myself, Jimmy Smart is at our backdoor. Telling Dreama good evening. Last of the light hung about his amber-coloured hair. His face stern. Dreama stubs out her Woodbine. Gets up from the table and slips past. Turns and tells us she's a mind to be out in the field alone. Barefoot, I know she'll turn there around and around until darkness has settled all over. Alone, I gaze at the showman, him three good paces away. His eyes flint black and sharp. Without uttering a sound, as if like Adie Lovekin my voice has been taken, I leave the kitchen. Drift through the coolness of the hall and upstairs. All the while aware the showman is just behind. In my bedroom he keeps quiet too. His gaze glances from me to the pile of stones and back again. As though he has a desire to boot the stones across the floor. Instead, he takes out a small silver tin from his pocket. Unscrews the lid and holds it beneath my nose. The balm is heady with herbs. Same as those Dreama and my mother would gather before the flood. Tells me it will help to make it hurt less. We undress hurriedly. My clothes left unfolded. Hands hasty and everywhere at once. Until he is red-faced and sweating. My own skin burning. He turns me around. Pushes me down onto the bed. My breath caught in the tangled sheet while he smears my arsehole with the balm until it's slick. Pushes his fingers inside of me. Then Jimmy Smart fucks me, his breath ragged, legs unsteady, toppling the pile of stones.

Did the field not want you tonight? I say.

Not so much, Dreama says.

I see.

He's gone then?

Yes—

Pity. I wanted to ask him about his Esme.

What 'bout her?

Out in the field I got to thinking. The pendulum I found. By the roadside. Might be it belonged to Adie Lovekin.

Doubt it.

Jimmy Smart's Esme would know.

Maybe—but he'll not ask her. She's been sick.

That so?

With a fever. Besides—Adie Lovekin isn't missing
any longer.

I know that.

And the two of us—are back on speaking terms.
Like you—wanted.

You don't suppose this sickness is catching?

Why'd you ask?

Look like you have a fever yourself.

Just the heat is all.

If you say so, Dreama says.

I do, I say.

The moon, that has been bright in the days before, is missing. Giving me the feeling that everything eventually goes
someplace else. With the line of light beneath Dreama's
bedroom door no longer, I slip past. Down dark stairs and
out to the waiting field. With warm dirt beneath bare feet,
I head for the yellow glow radiating from the middle. A
patch of dirt where the grass doesn't care to grow. Where I
find Jimmy Smart is on his back, hands cradling his head.

Bare-chested in just his underdrawers. He is something else to gaze on. In lamp light his skin a peculiar colour I've no name for. Glimmering. His smile pulls me down alongside him. Down on the rough blanket. Behind his head a scatter of moths gather against the glass lantern, beating their wings madly. Around us the field is alive with night noises, because we have disturbed the sleeping grass by being here at this hour. Jimmy Smart rolls onto his side. I suppose to get a better look at me. And I wonder if he knows I'm still giddy from earlier in my bedroom. Before he pulled on his clothes hastily and left like a sudden gust of wind. Me with an itchy neck where his beard had rubbed and growled. Our semen stirred together on my belly. Not wanting to wipe it away with my underdrawers. Though I did. Dressed myself and combed my hair smooth. Returned to the kitchen and put myself at the table, until Dreama returned from the field. Now, Jimmy Smart lights two Woodbines in his usual manner, handing me the spare. The smoke whirls around us, before disappearing into otherness as he starts talking of the fair. Him hating it deep down. His worry for Esme's peculiar fever. Both brothers, Tanner and Alick. How they're faring now he's a runaway. Then those two lions pacing back and forth in their cage. Ezzah and Afreen. Finding himself in the same predicament, before his old man went and killed them dead. Right away I can see that same storm gathering between his ears whenever he talks about them. Big enough to bend the grass sideways. Maybe even blow out the lantern. Because I want to tell him something that matters, but don't have the words, I take hold of his hand. To tug him away from the roof of their cage where he'd laid above them. Sometimes roaring. This whole time I believe Jimmy Smart has been alluding to him wanting to disappear. Same way my mother went

in the flood. I sit up, let loose Jimmy Smart's damp palm.
Because this disappearing scares me. Worse than any stone
that ever came booming through a windowpane.

You fixing on—leaving soon? I say.

Hadn't planned on it, Jimmy Smart says.

That's good.

Why? You and Dreama don't want me here
anymore?

No—nothing like that.

What then?

Was wondering is all.

Go on—

If you're not mad anymore? 'Bout me—calling you
a coward.

I'm working on it.

All right.

In the meantime, I've been thinking.

What 'bout?

Your Dreama and the field. Reckon you should rent
the land. If you don't want to plant it yourself.

Dreama won't hear of it.

Don't see why. Just hear me out. Cuz this way the farmers will be happy. Leave you be. And those goddamn stones'll stop busting through your windowpanes. Seems to me Dreama could use the money too.

She can't—rent the field. Not ever.

Why the hell not?

You—wouldn't understand, I say.

Then make me, Jimmy Smart says.

Dreama has found us. I don't know how long she's been here in the field at first light. Pale fingers clung to her collarbone. Her silk slip shimmering in the ebb and flow as she rocks. The grass isn't yet green, instead a quiet shade of blue. As though we're surrounded by water. A lake. And the banded blanket beneath us, the wooden boards of a boat. Might be I see want in her eyes. Chased by something else. I sit up. Pull my knees towards my chest to hide the bashfulness. I'd not noticed right away that my dick remains hard, a hazard of dreaming about the showman. I begin to open my mouth, to explain the situation, but Dreama lifts her finger to her lips and holds it there. Before turning and walking away towards the house. For a moment, I wonder if the field conjured her. Alongside me Jimmy Smart stirs. Rolls onto his back. Stretches and yawns like a lion might. Relief rushes through me when he grins, tugs at his underdrawers and sits up himself. Reaches behind for his packet of Woodbines. Taps one clear of the pack, lights it, and coughs madly. I watch the smoke drift. Then with no use for small talk, reminds me it's a workday. Collects the blanket into a rough bundle and makes for black barn. Turning back to see that I've collected the lantern. Outside black barn we take turns splashing our faces with water from the tin bucket. And Jimmy Smart runs a rag beneath his armpits. Disappears through the door. I follow behind, where he pulls on trousers and boots, leaving the laces untied, without a word between us. My own clothes are folded neatly inside the house. Yet I've little desire to fetch them. Until we hear the racket that is Shane Wright's motorcar coming down the dirt track. There's trouble in him being here. Jimmy Smart tells me to get back to the house. No use stirring things up worse than they are already. Inside the kitchen Dreama is sat at the table, smoking her Woodbine. I tell her Shane Wright is here, and she nods knowingly. Upstairs in my bedroom the stones are still scattered across the floorboards. A warning of what's waiting below. Making me feel disorientated. I dress hurriedly. Use water from the basin to flatten my hair before pulling a comb through. I wonder if I still smell of the showman, reluctant to use his rag before to wash his scent away. There's no time now. I tuck the tale of my shirt into the back of my trousers and go downstairs. Shane Wright is sat at the kitchen table where Dreama had been moments before. Hunched over. Jimmy Smart has his arms folded across his chest, back against the door, flung open to let the air crawl in. Still in just her slip Dreama puts down a glass of water before Shane Wright. And I step forward. Ask him what he's doing here at this hour on a workday. Because he has never set two steps inside this kitchen, or anywhere else nearby, on account of the cursed field. We watch him slug the glass dry. His skin appears bluer than I have ever seen. It's more than his beard growing through. Instead, bruises beneath his eyes as if he's stared into the sun for too long without blinking. Then his gaze travels around the room. Fixing on Jimmy Smart, who's unbuttoning his shirt in the heat. He nods, encouraging him to get on with his story. The day's waiting for him outside. Shane Wright looks like he might start sobbing. Though tells us he slept in his motorcar the night past. That in the hours before, two men in uniform came and took him. Because of the disappearing. Dreama tucks a length of yellow hair behind her ear. Jimmy Smart frowns. I pull out a chair and sit down. Because he means Adie Lovekin. Though it's Dreama who says the girl's name out loud. All at once Shane Wright is up and darting for the door, toppling his chair, where he disappears through the rectangle of light. We hear him heave and vomit onto the dirt outside. While Jimmy Smart is wanting to know what in the hell are we to do about it.

You can't mean it, I say.

Law suspects I took Adie Lovekin. Honest to God, Shane Wright says.

Doesn't—make any sense.

They kept on and on. All morning and into afternoon. Talking like I'm sick or something. Before they told me I could go. Though not far.

But—it's not true.

I know that.

They've made—a mistake is all.

The girl ain't helping none. Her not being able to speak.

I can't—hardly believe it.

Me neither.

What will you do?

That's why I'm here. I don't know what to do. You reckon I need a lawyer?

Might be you do.

Jesus.

Did you tell the law—

What?

That you're like me?

What, and have 'em arrest me for being a pervert?

Don't say that.

Why? It's what we are.

It won't help any—thinking like that.

Even if it's true, Shane Wright says.

But it's not, I say.

When the stone booms through the windowpane, slicing the skin beneath my left eye, I wonder if God is punishing me for fornicating with the showman. Shane Wright too.

Who sits behind bars this night, while Jimmy Smart is circling the house, hollering like a madman in the half-light. Might be more than retribution. More than our cursed field even. Before the broken window, Dreama had been gazing at the pendulum turning around and around, one way, then another. Casting a clever shadow. Now she is holding a cloth hard against my cheek to still the blood. Cursing because behind my head a vase she cared for has toppled and broken. This is preferable to her going on and on about her pendulum. She believes belonged to Adie Lovekin before the flood. That she can feel this truth, bone deep. This revelation and the past two days have stirred in me a tiredness unlike any other. An anger too. As Shane Wright has been imprisoned for taking Adie Lovekin. Refusing to tell the law the truth. What he really is. When Jimmy Smart comes back inside, claiming the culprit could be a ghost, I push Dreama's hand away. The cloth is ruined, more red than white. She tells the showman it looks worse than it is. That the scar will be nothing much at all. And hearing this I'm suddenly disappointed. That my scar will be nothing like Jimmy Smart's. Pale and sickle-shaped. Not a war wound collected during National Service. Instead, put there after an unruly wooden horse, driven by steam, had thrown him sideways. These conjured beasts that snort and kick and gallop, around and around. I remind myself to ask him if it were the grey horse. Because that would mean something. Though not now, as his face is troubled. His gaze absent. Still riled from the stone. Another to place on the pile at the foot of my bed. Without a word he turns around and goes back out the kitchen door. I help Dreama clear away the glass. Gather the pieces of her vase. When Jimmy Smart returns he is holding the silver tin. Tells me to sit myself down. Unscrews the lid, taking his time. Collects a finger full of balm, and rubs it across my sore cheek. His spare palm cradling my chin. Beneath the tabletop my dick threatens to disrupt my underdrawers. His hands are clever like that. After he's finished mending me, Dreama tells us she has a mind to make tea. That would we walk the field first. To be certain. Jimmy Smart nods. Outside, the last of the light glimmers. Before long, we find ourselves in the middle of the field. Put our backsides against the dirt here. Ahead of us is an indigo mountain that isn't really real. Though pretty just the same. Jimmy Smart lights us a Woodbine a piece. Sitting here, I'm restless with a feeling I've no name for. A feeling for the showman. Something other than desire. A familiarity. As if he is here on purpose. Then Jimmy Smart tells me we should sleep in the field tonight. On the blanket. That black barn is hotter than hell. He's right too.

Eli Stone— You ever gonna tell me the truth about this field? Cuz I know this dirt was cursed way before the flood went around it, Jimmy Smart says.

That's true, I say.

Reckon I've a right to know.

Dreama might believe otherwise.

She's gone mad with her pendulum turning. Doubt she'll care one way or the other.

I promised Dreama. And my mother.

You not trust me?

It's not that. I'm restless.

What about?

Shane Wright. Him not telling the truth of the situation.

It's a terrible thing. Though I don't see what can be done. Reckon it's better to be in prison for something he didn't do. Than the other.

You saying truth can be cunning?

Something like that.

If I tell you, you'll promise me something first?

And what might that be?

A ride on your grey horse.

I promise you the gallopers.

The curse is buried beneath us.

You're fooling me?

It's the truth. Where you going?

To get a shovel, Jimmy Smart says.

I wouldn't do that if I were you, I say.

1988

THE GALLOPERS

A PLAY

ELI STONE

CHARACTERS

(IN ORDER OF APPEARANCE)

ELIZA   *forty years old and wild.*

DREAMA *Eliza's younger sister.*

SHANE   *Dreama's son, seventeen.*

CLIFF   *Eliza's ex-boyfriend.*

ADIE   *Eliza's daughter.*

PLACE

A field beneath a wild Norfolk sky, ten miles from anywhere, during a sweltering day: August 1988. The field is ruined, with freshly dug holes all over the place. In the distance there's an iron bridge crossing an unseen river, ELIZA and DREAMA have swum in since childhood.

Also onstage is black barn, hunkered down and chaotic with twenty years of boxes and belongings, leaking onto the edge of the field. During World War Two ELIZA and DREAMA's mother stored black-market goods in a hole beneath the dirt floor.

When actors enter, they either enter from black barn or from the left, giving the impression of the house beyond the field.

ACT ONE

SCENE ONE

> *The sound of a merry-go-round blares out before the lights come up. As they do, the fairground music fades. We find ELIZA in the field, afternoon of a sweltering day. Her hair shorn short and coloured more yellow than blonde, arms outstretched, turning in circles. All the while DREAMA looks on, hands on her hips. Two sisters who are nothing alike.*

DREAMA: You hear me?

> *ELIZA turns faster.*

DREAMA: How many more holes you fixing to dig?

ELIZA: What's it matter? Besides, don't you hear that?

> *DREAMA comes closer, reaches out to still ELIZA.*

ELIZA: The horses!

DREAMA: I don't hear anything. Except maybe the train.
    Maybe—

ELIZA: You really can't hear the horses? Galloping nowhere.
    But inside, right here, it feels like somewhere. You know?

DREAMA: Sun's turned you stupid.

> SHANE *comes out of black barn with a heavy box*
> *that he dumps on the ground.*

DREAMA: Would you look at her. Might be heatstroke.

SHANE: (*to* ELIZA) You're all right I reckon.

ELIZA: Except—I'm fucking dying.

> *And stops turning.*

SHANE: You have to say it like that?

> *Folds his arms across his chest.*

ELIZA: It's the truth.

> SHANE *kicks a box of rubbish and goes back inside*
> *black barn.*

DREAMA: See what you did?

ELIZA: Be a whole lot faster if you'd help.

DREAMA: I'll not move one piece of dirt. You're acting crazy!

> *She gets down on her knees and tugs open the box*
> SHANE *dumped down before.*

ELIZA: What the hell you even doing?

DREAMA: Doesn't matter.

> ELIZA *lights a John Player Special. Blows blue smoke all about.*

DREAMA: My god—you remember this?

> *Holds up the hood of their mother's pink table-top hairdryer.*

ELIZA: Jesus Christ!

DREAMA: Was sure one day she'd set herself on fire.

ELIZA: Wish she had. Burned the whole damn house down with her.

DREAMA: You can't say that. Here—give me one of those.

ELIZA: Now who has heatstroke?

> *Hands* DREAMA *her cigarette and lights another for herself.*

DREAMA: God I miss smoking.

ELIZA: Then—why'd you quit?

DREAMA: For Shane. So he wouldn't pick up my bad habits.

ELIZA: And how'd that go?

> DREAMA *glares at* ELIZA.

ELIZA: How he is— You know what's going on with him, isn't a habit.

DREAMA: I know that.

ELIZA: Do you?

> DREAMA *sighs.*

ELIZA: You better had. Or—

DREAMA: Go on. Say it.

ELIZA: You'll lose him. He'll take off. It's in him. See it plain as dirt.

DREAMA: He's not like you.

> *Blows blue smoke at* ELIZA.

ELIZA: Isn't he?

DREAMA: Besides, where's he gonna go?

ELIZA: Anyplace is better than here.

DREAMA: And yet here you are. You've been back five minutes. You don't know anything. Because you haven't been around.

ELIZA: And you'll never not remind me.

DREAMA: Forget about it.

> ELIZA *flicks the rest of her cigarette into the hole beside her feet.*

DREAMA: Guess this is rubbish—too.

> *Puts the pink dryer hood back into the cardboard box.*

DREAMA: You remember when you cut off all my hair?

ELIZA: How could I forget? She went fucking nuts. But, I
    liked you before—

DREAMA: Before?

ELIZA: Doesn't matter.

DREAMA: No. It does.

ELIZA: Before you stopped being—

DREAMA: What?

ELIZA: You were something different back then. That's all
    I'm saying.

DREAMA: That's unfair.

ELIZA: Nothing's fucking fair.

DREAMA: You would say that.

ELIZA: Because it's the truth.

DREAMA: Well, I don't see how digging these goddamn holes
    is helping anyone.

    Waves her arms around.

    SHANE *comes out of black barn with another
    cardboard box.*

SHANE: (*to* DREAMA) You look like a scarecrow.

DREAMA: Don't be a smartarse.

SHANE: This one looks promising.

    Stands the box on the dirt.

ELIZA: What in the hell are the two of you looking for?

SHANE: Could ask you the same thing.

DREAMA: Never mind.

SHANE: (at ELIZA) Her albums. We're looking for her stupid photograph albums.

ELIZA: Why would anyone want them?

SHANE: That's what I said.

> DREAMA *sighs.*

SHANE: Err, what you digging for then?

> DREAMA *shakes her head.*

ELIZA: Treasure. Of course.

SHANE: I'm not an idiot.

> *Folds his arms across his chest.*

DREAMA: Then don't act like one.

SHANE: What'd I do?

ELIZA: You didn't do anything. Here—

> *Passes* SHANE *the packet of cigarettes from her pocket.*

DREAMA: Thought I said—

SHANE: Calm down, Mum. One cigarette won't kill me.

> ELIZA *laughs loudly.*

SHANE *lights his cigarette.*

SHANE: You gonna tell me. Or what?

ELIZA: (*to* DREAMA) Go on. Tell him.

DREAMA: A bomb. All right. She's digging holes all over our goddamn field looking for a bomb.

SHANE: You're fooling me?

ELIZA: It's the truth.

SHANE: A bomb?

DREAMA: (*sighs*) My whole goddamn life I've been hearing about that bomb. Sick to my teeth with it. You're as crazy as she was.

SHANE: Who?

ELIZA: Your grand—mother.

DREAMA: You don't have to say it like that.

ELIZA: Like what?

DREAMA: As though it tastes bad.

ELIZA: It does. But—

SHANE: (*interrupts*) Err, the holes! This bomb!

DREAMA: Fell before we were born. Nineteen-forty-one she said. Heard the plane. Went outside and there it was. Looking like a big blackbird soaring across the sky. She hated blackbirds. Couldn't stand the goddamn sight of them. Then it fell. The bomb. Whining like a kettle. That's what she always said. Just like a kettle.

SHANE: (*shrugs*) Our kettle doesn't whine.

DREAMA: Never mind.

SHANE: Wait! What happened afterwards?

DREAMA: Nothing.

SHANE: Who'd she tell? She must have said something to someone?

DREAMA: (*shakes her head*) Not a soul.

SHANE: No one!

DREAMA: That's what I said. She took a shovel and filled in the hole. Afterwards, believed the field must be cursed.

SHANE: Why'd she do that? What if it blew up!

ELIZA: Because she was fucking crazy.

SHANE: And now you're looking for it. That's mad.

ELIZA: (*nods*) I ain't digging these holes for nothing. That's for sure.

DREAMA *sighs.*

SHANE: But—it doesn't make sense.

ELIZA: Who says it has to?

SHANE: She's right. You are crazy.

ELIZA: Maybe I am. But it'll be fast. And big. I'll be in a
thousand tiny pieces. This fucking virus gone from me.
And—no one will ever know I was even here.

DREAMA: I'll know. You'll be spread all over the goddamn
windowpanes.

> ELIZA *laughs loudly.*

> SHANE *storms off back into black barn.*

DREAMA: See what you did?

ELIZA: Better he knows now. The truth of it.

DREAMA: He's seventeen.

ELIZA: That's plenty old enough.

DREAMA: Maybe you're right. But sometimes the truth
isn't—

ELIZA: What?

DREAMA: Who does it help?

ELIZA: (*shouts*) Me. It fucking helps me!

DREAMA: (*shakes her head*) I know what would help you.

ELIZA: Told you already. I won't talk 'bout that.

DREAMA: No—but you'll shoot your mouth off about everything else. Like you always have. Since we were girls. Not
caring one bit.

*ELIZA undoes the clasp on the chain around her
neck. There's a ring hung there.*

DREAMA: What you doing now?

*ELIZA holds out the chain before her, watches the
ring swing back and forth.*

ELIZA: Dowsing! How'd you think I'm deciding where to dig?

DREAMA: This heat's turned you mad. Don't see how it can
be so goddamn hot and still the wind is blowing. I smell
like the dog. You wanna go out to the bridge? Bet the
water's real cool. We could go skinny-dipping. Like we
used to.

ELIZA shakes her head, and keeps on dowsing.

DREAMA: (*sighs*) Then put that back on. And go and talk to
him. Please—

ELIZA: And say what exactly?

DREAMA: I don't know. That it'll be all right.

ELIZA: But—it won't.

DREAMA: Then just goddamn lie.

ELIZA fastens the chain around her neck.

ELIZA: I'll talk to him. But I won't lie.

ELIZA *goes inside black barn, and leaves DREAMA stood in the field alone, who stands and gazes at a scatter of blackbirds.*

(Blackout.)

SCENE TWO

Inside black barn ELIZA finds SHANE sat on a wooden crate, smoking one of her John Player Specials. He's taken off his t-shirt because it's sweltering inside. There's open boxes all over the place, their contents tipped out, looking like a bomb's gone off. ELIZA is unmoved by her childhood possessions littered about. Like they mean nothing at all. Because they don't.

ELIZA: (*to SHANE*) You ever planning on giving me those back?

Nods at the pack of cigarettes on the box beside him.

SHANE is shy all of a sudden about his bare chest. Folds and unfolds his arms.

SHANE: Err, here you go.

ELIZA: Dreama's right. You're all grown up.

SHANE: It's been two whole years.

ELIZA: You fooling?

SHANE: Bet my life on it.

ELIZA: You don't wanna be doing that.

SHANE: Sorry. Didn't mean anything by it.

> SHANE *goes over to the open window and flicks the rest of his cigarette out. Then sits back down.*

SHANE: Guess—I am grown up.

ELIZA: You know, there's a big fucking hole in the dirt, right beneath where you're sitting?

SHANE: Who gives a shit?

> ELIZA *opens her mouth, but no noise comes out.*

SHANE: What's with you and these holes?

ELIZA: My own goddamn mother used it during the war. For hiding cigarettes and black-market shit!

SHANE: For real?

ELIZA: (*shrugs*) Sometimes—I don't believe it, either. War is clever like that. Turning people into something they weren't before. You know—when I was your age, we used to hide our weed there. Would sneak out and smoke it over by the window.

SHANE: You and my mum?

ELIZA: (*nods*) Me and your mum. She wasn't always like she is—now.

SHANE: Now I know you're lying.

ELIZA: Cross my heart.

SHANE: Yeah— What was she like?

ELIZA: Bold. And beautiful. Everyone thought she'd be something big. Like a film star. The way she looked and all. Almost every boy 'round these parts was chasing after her— She was something else all right.

SHANE: Err, I don't wanna know that stuff.

ELIZA: You asked.

SHANE: (*shrugs*) Might be why she has me hunting for those stupid albums.

ELIZA: Sounds like Dreama. She'd carry that damn Brownie of hers everywhere. Always wanting a picture. Dunno why she quit taking 'em. Guess she went and grew out of it, is all. You remind me of her, you know? How she was back when we were your age. Everything in her head spilling straight out of her mouth. She was fearless.

SHANE: (*chin jutted out*) Nah, I'm not fearless. I take after my old man.

ELIZA: You do look like him, that's for sure. Just as handsome. But you're a smartarse too. And that you definitely get from your mum.

SHANE: And you!

　　　ELIZA *laughs loudly.*

SHANE: Maybe I am—a little bit fearless.

ELIZA: You wanna tell me what's going on with you?

SHANE: She send you in here? To ask me? It's no big deal.

> ELIZA *taps out a cigarette from her packet of John Play Specials and lights up.*

ELIZA: I was talking 'bout before in the field. The holes— You're mad at me.

SHANE: Nah. I don't wanna talk about that.

ELIZA: Then—we don't have to.

SHANE: You mean it?

ELIZA: Sure.

SHANE: That was easy.

ELIZA: How'd you mean?

SHANE: Mum would've banged on until my ears bled or something. She's always on my back these days.

ELIZA: I hear ya.

SHANE: (*shrugs*) She's angry. Nearly all the time. Like she's broken or something.

ELIZA: Yeah, I know. But it's not because of you.

SHANE: You reckon? Feels like it most days.

ELIZA: She worries 'bout you.

SHANE: There's no need to.

ELIZA: That you'll get hurt. Or—worse.

SHANE: What? Go on say it. That I'll get sick. Like you.

ELIZA *nods.*

SHANE: I can look after myself.

ELIZA: I don't doubt it. And what 'bout the windowpanes?

SHANE: What of 'em?

ELIZA: Dreama says there's been three broken this past
fortnight.

SHANE: It's nothing—

ELIZA: Doesn't seem like nothing.

SHANE: (*head down*) Just some local lads is all. Messing
around.

ELIZA: (*nods*) All right.

SHANE: (*big pause*) I fucking hate them—

ELIZA: I'm—

SHANE: Don't say you're sorry. Anything but that.

ELIZA: I'm—fucking furious.

SHANE *laughs a little.*

SHANE: If they keep at it, reckon I'll clear off. Go stay with
my old man.

ELIZA: He know what you are?

SHANE *hops up off the wooden crate, paces back and
forth a bit. Then kicks a battered tin bucket across
the floor, that zooms through the open door.*

91

SHANE: Who cares?

ELIZA: I meant—

SHANE: And what fucking difference does it make? To him? You? Nobody's business but my own.

> ELIZA *gets up, goes over to the open window and tosses the half-smoked cigarette out.*

ELIZA: (*to the field*) He'll figure you out sooner or later. They always do—

SHANE: Huh?

> ELIZA *goes over to* SHANE.

ELIZA: I care 'bout you.

SHANE: No you don't. Else you wouldn't be digging out there in the field. Looking for some stupid bomb. I don't want you to die.

> SHANE *hugs* ELIZA. *Then let's go just as fast.*

ELIZA: Me neither.

SHANE: Then stop digging already.

ELIZA: It's complicated.

SHANE: That's something Mum says a lot.

> ELIZA *laughs loudly.*

ELIZA: Like every other seventeen-year-old, you'll understand some day.

SHANE: But, I'm not like every other seventeen-year-old, am I? I'm bent.

ELIZA: I hate that word.

SHANE: Thing is—maybe I don't hate it.

ELIZA: But—

SHANE: (interrupts ELIZA) What I'm saying—is I'm sort of all right. Maybe I wanna be different (folds and unfolds his arms).

ELIZA: I ever tell you how brave you are?

SHANE: Stop messing.

ELIZA: I mean it. Bravest person I know. Cross my heart.

> ELIZA smiles. Then reaches over to an open box. Pulls out a bar of cream-coloured soap.

ELIZA: Why in hell would anyone keep a used bar of soap?

SHANE: (shrugs) Beats me.

> (Blackout.)

SCENE THREE

> ELIZA has returned to the field alone, where she's taken off her chain, dowsing for the next hole to dig. SHANE and DREAMA are inside the house. CLIFF, ELIZA's ex-boyfriend from way before, has driven from town to repair the windowpanes, and discovers

ELIZA has returned home. CLIFF is still handsome as hell, and wears cut-offs and a t-shirt that's two sizes too small for him.

CLIFF: Hey stranger.

ELIZA turns around, smiles, because she'd recognise CLIFF's voice anywhere.

ELIZA: Dreama tell you—I'm back?

Fastens the chain around her neck.

CLIFF: (*nods*) She did. But I know any day you'd have called to tell me. That my ring around your neck?

ELIZA: It is— And I would have called—

CLIFF: Liza girl. You look good. I mean—even that hair!

ELIZA runs fingers through her short, shorn hair.

ELIZA: Dreama cut it for me. You like it?

CLIFF: It's hot!

ELIZA laughs loudly.

ELIZA: Bullshit.

CLIFF: Honest to God.

And makes the sign of the cross on his chest, all the while he grins.

CLIFF: I gotta know. Dreama never tells me the good stuff. But—what in the hell are all these holes? It's crazy as those broken windowpanes back there.

ELIZA: (shrugs) Trust me. You don't wanna know.

CLIFF: Guess some things never change. Except maybe your hair.

> ELIZA stands still and smiles. Because she's glad to see him.

CLIFF: What's up?

ELIZA: Nothing. It's good to see you is all.

CLIFF: How long you back for?

ELIZA: For good. I guess.

> CLIFF folds his arms across his chest.

CLIFF: Doesn't sound like you.

ELIZA: No?

CLIFF: (shakes his head) Uh uh.

ELIZA: Don't you have windowpanes to fix?

CLIFF: Now you're in a hurry to get rid of me? Not one minute ago you were telling me—how good I looked.

ELIZA: That's not what I said.

CLIFF: Yeah—it was.

> ELIZA shrugs.

CLIFF: Besides, I ain't in any kind of hurry.

ELIZA: You're right. Some things never change.

CLIFF: Now that's not very friendly.

ELIZA: Could be by the time you walk up to the house, another pane'll be broken.

CLIFF: If I catch one of them bastards hurling stones, I'll beat the crap out 'em.

ELIZA: Dreama tell you?

CLIFF: (*frowns*) She did.

ELIZA: You have any idea who it might be?

CLIFF: Some. You know what townies are like.

ELIZA: Sure do—

CLIFF: I tell ya— That lad's in for a world of trouble.

ELIZA: How'd you know 'bout Shane?

CLIFF: (*shrugs*) I ain't blind, Liza. Figured it out fortnight past. The way the lad was watching me climb up and down the ladder all morning. His tongue hanging out. I'd seen that same look on my own face when I was seventeen in the bathroom mirror.

> CLIFF *takes out a packet of cigarettes, taps two free, lights them up and passes ELIZA the spare.*

> ELIZA *takes a drag of her cigarette. Blows blue smoke about.*

CLIFF: He's harmless.

ELIZA: I know that.

CLIFF: He getting ready to run or something?

ELIZA: How'd you mean?

CLIFF: Seems to me he'd be better off someplace bigger. Instead of this small town. Find lads like himself. I reckon he has that look in his eye. Same one you had— about to take off any minute.

ELIZA: (*shrugs*) Dreama's worried he will. Worried he won't. I dunno.

CLIFF: (*sighs*) Well Dreama can't keep paying for window-panes. They ain't cheap to fix.

    ELIZA *nods*.

CLIFF: You want me to have a word with Shane?

ELIZA: You'd do that?

CLIFF: Might be he'll give up their names. Can have a word with 'em if he does.

ELIZA: All right.

CLIFF: (*grins*) Now we've taken care of that. You gonna tell me what in the hell you're doing out here? What's with the holes? There must be—twenty by my count!

ELIZA: Don't reckon you'll wanna hear it.

CLIFF: When have I never not been interested in what you have to say?

    ELIZA *shrugs*.

ELIZA: It's different now.

CLIFF: Why'd people always say that. Sounds stupid to me.

ELIZA: I guess, because it's true.

CLIFF: Not to me. We ain't together or nothing. But we're still friends aren't we?

ELIZA: (nods) Always—

> CLIFF flicks the rest of his cigarette into the field. Clears his throat.

CLIFF: So shoot.

> ELIZA looks over her shoulder at twenty heaps of dirt. Figures there's no way around it. Then back at CLIFF, who gazes and waits for the truth.

ELIZA: Just realised it. But—these holes look like little graves.

CLIFF: (shrugs) Suppose they do.

ELIZA: I'd tell ya to sit down if I thought it'd do any good.

CLIFF: I'm just fine standing.

ELIZA: There's no easy way to say it. I'm sick—

CLIFF: I know. I ain't here by accident.

ELIZA: Goddamn Dreama. There anything she hasn't told ya?

CLIFF: (*shakes his head*) Never the good stuff, remember! Though you don't look sick to me. Or behaving like someone who's sick.

ELIZA: How's someone who's sick meant to behave?

Flicks the rest of her cigarette into the field.

CLIFF: I don't know. In bed and shit.

ELIZA: I'm—dying Cliff.

CLIFF walks back and forth a bit. Undecided how to handle ELIZA's proclamation.

CLIFF: Don't say it out loud. Was bad enough hearing Dreama say it before. Her as miserable as a person can be.

CLIFF rushes forward and takes hold of ELIZA, hugs her hard.

CLIFF: (*lets go*) There's new drugs though. Dreama—

ELIZA: Doesn't know shit. If she did that'd at least be something.

CLIFF: How can you joke about it?

ELIZA: If I didn't—I'd go fucking insane.

CLIFF: You hurting. I mean, is it painful?

ELIZA: Not so much.

CLIFF nods.

ELIZA: Besides, Dreama's taking good care of me.

CLIFF: Yeah? Can't imagine that's going too well.

> ELIZA *laughs loudly.*

ELIZA: You know Dreama. Even dying I'm pissing her off.

CLIFF: Jesus—

> CLIFF *takes* ELIZA'*s cheeks in his big palms. Leans in to kiss her.*

ELIZA: (*pulls away*) Don't!

CLIFF: It's all right. I can't catch—

ELIZA: (*shouts*) Fuck you!

CLIFF: I'm sorry Liza.

ELIZA: Everyone's fucking sorry all the time.

CLIFF: It'll be all right.

ELIZA: Yeah? You can't even say the word. How will it ever be all right?

CLIFF: (*frowns*) AIDS. There, I said it.

> ELIZA *sighs, looks behind her at the little graves everywhere, then back at* CLIFF.

ELIZA: You need to leave Cliff. I know you better than anyone. What's beneath that pleasing smile of yours. Those goddamn eyes I don't want gazing at me. I know what's in your head. Can see it turning around and around. Trying to figure a way out.

CLIFF: That's hardly fair.

ELIZA: I keep hearing that lately.

CLIFF: I'm asking for a chance, that's all.

ELIZA: I'm all out of chances.

> ELIZA *points to the house past black barn and keeps her arm out until* CLIFF *turns around and walks away.*

> *(Blackout.)*

SCENE FOUR

> ELIZA *digs in the field. Amongst more holes than when* CLIFF *walked away to mend the windowpanes at the house. The sound of the merry-go-round blares out again.* ELIZA *is wet with sweat and worn out. Though she keeps on. Rattled by the fairground music and the sound of horses neighing and kicking and galloping, until interrupted by* DREAMA.

DREAMA: You carry on like this and you won't need to find no damn bomb. You'll be dead anyway.

> ELIZA *just gazes at* DREAMA.

DREAMA: Here.

> *Passes* ELIZA *a can of pop.*

> ELIZA *pulls the ring and drinks the can dry.*

DREAMA: (*swats at the air*) These damn ladybirds all over the place. Crawling everywhere! You remember the beach that time? Never seen so many. Must have been a million. Like the sand was bleeding or something.

ELIZA: I'm not speaking to you.

DREAMA: (*sighs*) Someone had to tell Cliff.

ELIZA: None of his business.

DREAMA: (*ignores* ELIZA) Look! You've two on your arm.

> ELIZA *brushes the ladybirds away.*

DREAMA: Maybe it's a sign?

ELIZA: Doesn't mean nothing. You think everything means something.

DREAMA: Because it does. Things don't just happen for no good reason.

ELIZA: Then how'd you explain this!

> *Opens out her arms, like she's beneath the big top, about to announce the lion tamer.*

> DREAMA *sighs.*

ELIZA: Besides, them ladybirds weren't so lucky on the beach that day. Getting stomped all over.

DREAMA: You got me there. I didn't come out here to fight.

ELIZA: Could've fooled me.

DREAMA: Figured you would've had enough of that—after Cliff. Came back before mad as hell. Like his backside was on fire. Why'd you rile him up like that? He kicked the glass he'd set out to pieces!

ELIZA: (*shrugs*) That so?

DREAMA: Took Shane with him to town.

ELIZA: Shane all right with that?

DREAMA: Reckon so. Two of them came back an hour later in better shape than when they rode off. They fixed one windowpane before heading to the river to cool off.

ELIZA *nods.*

DREAMA: I had to tell Cliff. He's the only one you ever listened to. I thought maybe he could convince you—eventually.

ELIZA: Told you already. I don't wanna talk 'bout that.

DREAMA: Jesus you're stubborn. Just like her.

ELIZA: Leave our mother out of it.

DREAMA: (*shakes her head*) How can I? When you're out in the damn field digging holes all over the place. I hate this field some days. Have since I was a girl. You remember the flood? I know we were just small girls. But I can still hear the water running everywhere but here. Her saying the field was cursed. When I—thought we'd been spared.

ELIZA: I remember. Like we were being punished. She was—fucked up.

DREAMA: She told me once, ours was the field God forgot.

ELIZA: I didn't know that.

DREAMA: How could you?

ELIZA: (*shrugs*) And you're wrong. I'm nothing like her.

DREAMA: Prove it. Go easy on Cliff. That's all I'm asking.

ELIZA: And why would I do that?

DREAMA: Because he cares about you.

ELIZA: He'll get over it.

DREAMA: Do you have to be such a cunt?

>ELIZA *kicks the shovel to the dirt.*

ELIZA: You don't get to talk to me like that. I don't owe Cliff a damn thing.

DREAMA: I'm your sister! And you do owe Cliff something. All of us!

ELIZA: What might that be?

DREAMA: The goddamn chance to care.

ELIZA: Told Cliff—I'm all out of chances.

DREAMA: Don't—

ELIZA: What?

DREAMA: (*sighs*) Make us miss you—while you're still here.

ELIZA *takes out her packet of John Player Specials,*
lights up two, and hands the spare to DREAMA.
Then ELIZA *takes hold of* DREAMA's *hand, just for a*
moment, and lets go.

DREAMA: You know what I'm thinking. I reckon she burned
those goddamn albums.

Motions towards black barn.

ELIZA: Be just like her. Why in the hell do you want 'em so
badly?

DREAMA: I don't know. Been thinking on things lately. Gets
me up in the night walking the floor. Last night the moon
looked like a dinnerplate licked clean.

ELIZA: It sure did!

DREAMA: You were awake too?

ELIZA: It's the damn heat. I came out to the field. Laid down
in the dirt over there. You know, I don't see how a bunch
of old pictures will help any.

DREAMA: You've not one sentimental bone in your
whole body.

ELIZA: (*shrugs*) That's true.

DREAMA: Our whole entire childhood are in those albums.

ELIZA: Where it belongs!

Laughs loudly.

DREAMA *sighs.*

DREAMA: Maybe you're right. But I wanna see just the same. What we looked like before everything got so—messed up. When we weren't—

ELIZA: What?

DREAMA: Such strangers.

> ELIZA *flicks the rest of her cigarette away.* DREAMA *takes one last drag, and does the same.*

DREAMA: You know, there'll be a picture of Adie in those albums somewhere?

ELIZA: You never listen. How many times?

DREAMA: I just don't see how you can't be thinking about her. With everything that's happening.

> ELIZA *puts her back to* DREAMA.

DREAMA: Someone has to say something. It's why you came home isn't it?

ELIZA: (*shakes her head*) You a fortune teller now?

DREAMA: I feel it inside.

> *Taps her chest.*

DREAMA: Same as I know you don't really wanna find that goddamn bomb.

> ELIZA *turns around, gazes at* DREAMA *for a long time.*

DREAMA: Don't you wanna see Adie?

ELIZA: What I want— (*pause*) What I want is for you to let it go, Dreama. Why'd you always have to drag up every bad thing that ever fucking happened to anyone? It's like an addiction or something.

DREAMA: That's not what I'm doing here.

ELIZA: Then what in the hell are you doing? Because this isn't helping. You! And now Cliff! This isn't something you can fix. I'm dying Dreama. Fucking dying!

> DREAMA *has tears in her eyes. She turns away to wipe her face.*

DREAMA: Well—you're not dead—yet.

> ELIZA *laughs loudly.*

ELIZA: (*then serious*) I just—

DREAMA: Go on.

ELIZA: (*shrugs*) It hurts. Like I'm on fire inside. All of the time. As if my fucking bones are kindling. I can't barely stand it some days.

DREAMA: What can I do?

> ELIZA *shakes her head.*

ELIZA: Nothing—

> DREAMA *looks up at the sky, like she might find a sign there.*

DREAMA: I don't know what to do.

ELIZA: Then don't do anything.

> SHANE and CLIFF enter stage left, after their swim beneath the iron bridge, their hair still damp. DREAMA takes hold of SHANE's arm, and they go inside black barn, leave CLIFF and ELIZA alone in the field.

ELIZA: You gonna stand there staring? Or say something?

CLIFF: I wanna help! Tell me what to do.

ELIZA: You got a metal detector in that van of yours?

CLIFF: Huh?

> CLIFF steps forward and hugs her hard. They stand in the field, together, while the sound of the merry-go-round builds.

> (Blackout.)

SCENE FIVE

> ELIZA and SHANE in black barn, after CLIFF cleared off back to the house. SHANE is bouncing after his swim out at the iron bridge before with CLIFF, telling ELIZA all about it. The light now is that magic time, in-between day and night, when everything glimmers. ELIZA sits and watches SHANE rummage through boxes looking for DREAMA's albums. Believing their mother really did burn them.

ELIZA: Glad Cliff's gone home.

SHANE: I wish he'd hung around! I like him.

ELIZA: (*shrugs*) Me too. It's just things with Cliff are—

SHANE: I know—complicated!

>   ELIZA *laughs loudly.*

ELIZA: You got it.

SHANE: He's cool.

ELIZA: He'd laugh if he heard you say that.

SHANE: How come?

ELIZA: It's the same as saying he's old!

SHANE: But he isn't.

ELIZA: (*shrugs*) That's true— Though he's a lot older than
>   you. I can see you're keen. He ask you 'bout the broken
>   windowpanes?

>   SHANE *shrugs.*

SHANE: I'm not a grass.

ELIZA: He's trying to help is all.

SHANE: I'll figure it out for myself.

ELIZA: (*nods*) How was the river? Right now I'm wishing I'd
>   gone with the two of you. This goddamn heat!

SHANE: (*shrugs*) Good—

>   ELIZA *fans herself with a piece of cardboard she's
>   picked up.*

SHANE: (*quiet*) I like looking at him.

ELIZA: You and most of the town! Better you should know now, men like him are a world of trouble.

SHANE: (*bashful*) I know he's not like me. I ain't stupid. But— he's not all weird around me. When we were swimming before, he didn't look at me like I'm a sissy or something.

ELIZA: Cliff's different from every other man I've known.

SHANE: How'd you mean?

ELIZA: He's unique.

> ELIZA *closes her eyes for a beat.*

ELIZA: And handsome as hell!

SHANE: (*nods*) Then how come the two of you ain't together? Out at the river, he ran on and on about you. Like you were his favourite word or something.

ELIZA: (*laughs loudly*) Is that so? You know what, too much of a good thing can be as bad as nothing at all.

SHANE: That's stupid.

ELIZA: You're right. But the women in our family have to be careful. Seems to me they get rubbed out even before they disappear. Might be why your mother's hunting for those albums. You'll need to watch out too.

SHANE: How'd you figure that? I ain't a woman!

ELIZA: Little smartarse! But—they'll be men someday who'll wanna do the same to you no doubt. Men are clever like that.

SHANE: (*grins*) Doesn't sound so bad to me!

> ELIZA *laughs loudly.*

ELIZA: (*looks around*) I don't reckon you'll ever find those albums.

SHANE: Try telling Mum that. Before, she was banging on about all the ladybirds flying around. One of her signs. She said—

> DREAMA *is a dark silhouette at the door. She has heard* ELIZA *and* SHANE *talk about* CLIFF.

DREAMA: You find them yet?

> SHANE *is startled.* ELIZA *doesn't even flinch.*

SHANE: Jesus, Mum! No—I haven't. Not yet.

ELIZA: Tomatoes need watering.

SHANE: I did it yesterday—

DREAMA: Go do it again. And mind the ladybirds.

> SHANE *sighs, leaves* ELIZA *and* DREAMA *in black barn. But they can hear him sing 'Fast Car' to himself on his way.*

> DREAMA *takes a spinning top out of a cardboard box nearby. The tin toy is worn and red, and has a scatter of blackbirds painted all around it.*

111

DREAMA: Haven't seen this in years.

ELIZA: (*shrugs*) Never seen it before. Whose was it?

> *Stands up and looks around at the mess of open boxes
> and rubbish all over the place.*

DREAMA: Yours—

ELIZA: (*ignores* DREAMA) Maybe we should just burn this
barn down?

> DREAMA *sighs.*

DREAMA: You and Shane are right. I don't think we'll find
those damn albums.

ELIZA: Starting to think the same thing 'bout that bomb!

DREAMA: For God's sake, Eliza!

ELIZA: (*shrugs*) Thought I'd found it before. Turned out to
be an old oil drum. What I need—is a metal detector. You
know anyone who has one?

DREAMA: Let me think—no of course not! Besides, I'll sleep
better knowing it's still beneath the dirt.

ELIZA: You'll sleep better when it's gone from the field all
together.

DREAMA: (*sighs*) How can you say that? If it means you'll be
gone too.

> ELIZA *shrugs.*

DREAMA: Maybe she made it up? That all along there's been nothing beneath the dirt except worms and flint. Be just like her. Sometimes, I wonder if one true thing ever left that woman's lips.

ELIZA: It's here somewhere.

DREAMA *hurls the tin spinning top against the wooden wall. Makes a big bang that startles* ELIZA.

ELIZA: What the hell Dreama?

DREAMA: (*sobs a little*) We do disappear. Don't we? I mean—

ELIZA: Huh?

DREAMA: What you told Shane before. About the women in this family. I was out there all the while listening to the two of you. And you're right—about all of it.

ELIZA: (*shrugs*) I didn't mean anything. Was just talking is all.

DREAMA *gazes at* ELIZA, *who taps out a cigarette from her packet of John Player Special, though the lighter won't spark. She tries over and over.*

DREAMA: (*loudly*) I wanna know his name.

ELIZA: What?

DREAMA: Tell me his goddamn name. So I know—

ELIZA *puts down the unlit cigarette and lighter.*

DREAMA: The man has to have a name!

ELIZA: (*shakes her head*) What difference will it make?

DREAMA: It matters to me. I wanna know who disappeared you. Tell me!

> ELIZA *gets up and goes over to* DREAMA, *takes hold of her hand.*

ELIZA: All right—his name was Jimmy.

DREAMA: Jimmy—

ELIZA: (*pause*) Jimmy Smart— Same as the name on the rounding boards above the ride.

DREAMA: (*thinks about it*) Ride?

ELIZA: He's a showman. Turning the gallopers. You can figure out the rest.

> DREAMA *sobs.*

DREAMA: I hate him. And those goddamn gallopers.

ELIZA: (*urgent*) Don't hate the horses. I hear them sometimes. Calling me—

> ELIZA *walks out of black barn.* DREAMA *follows behind. In the field* ELIZA *closes her eyes. Tips her head back towards the big sky above. There is the faint sound of the merry-go-round and horses gallop in half-light.*

ELIZA: You know—he told me the Italians that painted them, before the war, charmed the colour somehow. To make them more alive. Snorting and kicking and hurtling around and around. You believe that?

DREAMA: (*sighs*) I believe he charmed the hell out of you.

ELIZA: (*nods*) He did so much more than that Dreama.

DREAMA: I know—

ELIZA: He took it all. Every hope I've ever had. Every dream. Jimmy Smart killed me. Same as if he'd done it with his bare hands.

> ELIZA and DREAMA stand in the field amongst the holes, like little graves everywhere, while the sound of the merry-go-round blares out.
>
> (*Blackout.*)

1954

Casting a purple shadow on the frozen field I watch a pair of hungry blackbirds hammer the ground above the bomb. Jimmy Smart boots a rock, scaring the birds sky bound. A black blur against the sheet of white. Tells me he's not had one good night's sleep since the summer. Since I gave up the truth. When I'd convinced the showman to leave the bomb beneath the dirt. The shovel idle in black barn. I sigh. Because something else is on Jimmy Smart's mind these months past. Even after Dreama brought him in from black barn and his fold-out bed. On account of the cold weather coming in. Her not caring to utter a word about our sleeping together in my bed. An unspoken agreement now he's one of us. Knows the truth, and why we leave the field be. Still, he is restless. Scrapping alongside me in bed most nights like a welterweight might. The blue bruises I own are proof enough. All along my left side. I've a mind to trade places to give my ribs a rest. He's sorry when he sees me naked in first light. Runs rough fingers across them. Sometimes his special balm. Though we've near used the whole tin. Now Jimmy Smart's gaze is unguarded. This way he watches me when no one else is around. Except for the blackbirds that have returned. He passes me his half-smoked Woodbine, and pulls up the collar of my coat to keep the cold out. The wool is itchy. Smells like yesterday's stew. Then he threatens to haul me across the field to his motorcar, idling on the track. If I don't quit stalling. Wondering if there's a way around this situation. I blow blue smoke out, that hangs ahead of me as if it might freeze. I know there's no use arguing the matter and follow behind Jimmy Smart, whose stride is almost double my own. At the motorcar, I help clear the last of the ice from the windshield. Blowing on my fingertips afterwards, until the colour comes back. Climb inside. Where he drives down the track, unconcerned about the weather, out onto the road.

Out with it, Jimmy Smart says.

It's nothing, I say.

Now I know you're lying. Cuz nothing with you is never not something. I've not harmed you have I? In the night?

You haven't.

You're like this each time we set off for the Heath.

I don't mean to be.

I know.

If only Shane Wright would tell the truth.

Know what your Dreama would say—if wishes were horses.

I don't understand is all.

Cuz you don't care to.

What's that mean?

You know why Shane Wright won't tell the truth.

Guess I do. Doesn't mean I like it.

No one said you had to.

Some days I wish I'd never heard of Adie Lovekin.

We all do.

Dunno what to do 'bout it.

Nothing. Cuz he wants you to leave it be.

Dreama reckons there's a world of difference between what a person wants and needs.

That so?

Like two roads running in different directions.

You already know what I think about it, Eli.

I do, I say.

Then leave it be, Jimmy Smart says.

Instead of dwelling on Mousehold Heath and the prison there, where Shane Wright waits locked-up, I gaze at fields passing by. Though at once I'm reminded, even in winter, the land around here appears more abandoned than our own field. Winter crops absent from the ground. Five miles from here there's a line you'd likely miss if you weren't looking for it. Or not from around these parts. This line is something God might have left behind, dividing the dirt in two. On one side everything is as it should be. The other, unable to hold on to green after the flood. It hurts to go on gazing. On the inside of my eyelids I see the summer before. And long for the ice to thaw. Where I can climb the bank all the way up to iron tracks and hurl myself into the air. Fall through the surface beneath like a sinking stone. Knowing Jimmy Smart is there to watch over me. Which makes me ache worse for hiding why I'm not myself. It's more than us heading for the Heath to visit Shane Wright. The man they say took Adie Lovekin, and her voice. It's more too than Dreama and her damn pendulum. The two of them turning in circles around and around, going nowhere. Instead, the wet is on my mind. Stirring beneath my skin. As though that night is here again just now. Haunting me. Because it'll be one year tomorrow since the flood washed away my mother. When a great gale herded the water inland, everywhere but our field. As if something had a hand in it. Followed by our troubles with the farmers and their wives. The same people Dreama goes to church with. Knowing the hands that hurl the stones are amongst them. All at once I'm glad. Glad to be on the road with Jimmy Smart. Away from Dreama. The pile of stones that sits at the foot of my bed still. These things that threaten to dislodge everything I've tried so hard to hold on to. Somehow, seeing Shane Wright doesn't seem so bad. Where the guards look on at the three of us like we're something unnatural.

You burn them all, like I asked? Shane Wright says.

Every last one, I say.

Waste if you ask me. And stupid. Know I said I'd stay out of it. But if they'd have found 'em you wouldn't be sat here for taking that girl. Cuz they'd know what you are, and Eli wouldn't be on your back about telling the truth, Jimmy Smart says.

You mind if I talk to Eli alone?

Makes no difference to me.

He's right—'bout the magazines.

Leave it be.

Don't see how being what we are is worse than them believing you took Adie Lovekin.

I reckon it's worse. We've been over it. Again and again. You'll not change my mind.

All right.

You'll do something for me?

What?

Go to the gym.

Why'd you want me to do that?

Ask Bill Bredlau to come visit me. I've written. But he won't come, Shane Wright says.

I'll do it, I say.

Twins can be bewildering to gaze at. Standing on our track that's coloured more purple than grey in afternoon light. Huddled in dark winter coats. The wind knocking them together until they appear to be joined down the middle. Like something you might see at the circus. At once I'm wary. Even before Jimmy Smart tells me to stay put, while he gets out of the motorcar and walks on over. These must be the Smart Brothers, Tanner and Alick. Though I don't know what name belongs to which brother. I reckon they've come here today to take Jimmy Smart home. As he said they might. Reminded me again day before that the Mart rolls into Lynn in a fortnight's time. And I consider his rules that don't apply anywhere but there. The same rules he's been murmuring in his sleep these past months. Along with his brothers' names and holes in the ground. I watch through the windshield. At how unalike they seem. While Jimmy Smart's hair is amber and sprung, Tanner's is flat. Alick's too. Both pale as though winter wind has blown all colour away. Where Jimmy Smart is built like a welterweight, his brothers are heavier and a good bit taller. I know nothing much of these men. Or the way things are between them. Because Jimmy Smart won't talk about it. Then he's back at the motorcar. Opens the door and leans inside. Tells me to go on in the house while he talks with his brothers. On the walk past, they both nod. Unsettling me. If things weren't bad enough outside, there's more trouble here. Dreama stands by the table. Dazed and smoking her Woodbine. Ash collecting in her palm. The table itself is laid with people I've never known. Cabinet photographs all over until the silvered pine beneath has disappeared. I want to know how long the men have been standing around outside and she shrugs. An hour she believes. Maybe more. Returns her gaze to the photographs gathered after the flood, plucked from dark hedges, growing like leaves. Fifty or more. Their edges curled and water damaged. These people belong elsewhere. I don't want them here. One time I found a photograph of my mother's great uncle with his pretty wife and infant. Except the infant was something other than it appeared to be. Dead. My mother told me they made such photographs to remember. Since that day I've not cared for pictures. That's why I tell Dreama to clear the table. That I'll make us some tea. For her to put the photographs in a box and leave them at church. Where the Reverend can remind the congregation to take back their dead.

Wondered if you want me and Jimmy Smart to come to church tomorrow? I say.

Why'd you wanna go and do a thing like that? Shane Wright'll need more than prayers, Dreama says.

Not for him.

What then?

On account of—it's been one year.

I know that—

Suppose you do.

And since when has Jimmy Smart been the praying kind?

Since I asked him to come.

Suit yourselves.

That's decided then.

You making tea?

I am.

Think they'll want some? Those fellas outside.
It's bitter cold today. And that sky. You've seen it?
Before I was sure it looked—

Looks as plain as any other day, I say.

If you say so. Maybe I will take these pictures to
church tomorrow. Leave 'em there. Forget about the
tea. I'd sooner lie down. I've one of my headaches,
Dreama says.

With Dreama resting upstairs in her room, I peer through
the windowpane at black barn. Hunkered down beside the
field. I suppose Jimmy Smart took his brothers inside to get
away from the cold for a time. Wind too. When the whistle
blows I bang my brow against the pane. Take the kettle off
the flame. Return to before. The hole from the summer is
still there, patched with greaseproof paper, because Dreama
won't let the showman mend it properly. All at once they're
outside. Seems to me Tanner and Alick are unlike Jimmy
Smart in a way I don't understand. As if, like the gallopers,
they're part of the same merry-go-round. Yet carved from
different wood. Then past the house heading for the track,
where their motorcar is parked. While I wait for the showman, I gather up the photographs from the table that Dreama

left behind. There's relief that she'll take them to church in the morning. With us by her side. When he comes through the backdoor, he unbuttons his heavy coat and hangs it on the hook alongside mine. And Dreama's purple shawl. Comes over and sits across from me at the table. Lights a Woodbine. I pour hot water for tea, while he apologises for Tanner and Alick. Them being unable to come inside this day. Wants to know where Dreama has gone. Nodding when I tell him she has one of her headaches. Then he does something dangerous. His head tipped sideways. Takes out his silver tin and slides is slowly across the pine tabletop. Gets up. First he unties his boot laces, kicks free of the leather. Takes off his shirt. Trousers. Slides down his underdrawers. Until he's naked except for his brown socks. His dick, no longer swinging, juts out parallel to the floor, and might be the most distracting thing I've ever seen. Until my gaze travels up Jimmy Smart's belly. Following the line dissecting his chest. Past his Adam's apple. To his eyes. Darker than the day before, they study me. And right then I'm reminded of something I'd felt before in the summer. Known even. That Jimmy Smart is here on purpose. And another thing. His pleasing dick is more than it appears, a charm to captivate. Maybe he's been distracting me all along with his illusions. I know nothing for sure, when I take Jimmy Smart's dick into my mouth. That tastes like last night, and piss. Except this desire turning everything upside down, and a rush of agreeable noises filling my ears.

Cuz I ain't a liar, I need to say something, Jimmy Smart says.

Go ahead, I say.

Thing is—Tanner and Alick— They want me to come home.

Figured as much.

Season's starting up in a fortnight with Lynn Mart. Reckon things aren't going too good. Told me it was the same when I was away for two years. Two of 'em turning the gallopers without me means hiring a hand for another season. To them that's the same as throwing stones at the wind.

You—leaving then?

Truth is, I might have to. My brothers can be pretty persuasive. Don't matter that it's them telling the same old story—even my ears themselves were bored. There's rules.

Those stupid rules again.

Hold your horses. I ain't told 'em I will. Just that I'll think on it some.

Seems like you've made up your mind already.

It's complicated is all.

I reckon people are nothing but their big tales.

Where'd that come from?

Like a magic trick that has you looking south. When everything that matters is north of where you're standing.

You're talking crazy. Like Dreama.

Am I?

You are. Cuz I ain't trying to trick you Eli. And I don't make the rules, Jimmy Smart says.

Then don't follow them, I say.

The road to church is moody. More than the dark hedgerow beneath this white sky, hung like a bedsheet to dry. Jimmy Smart walks ahead, mumbling about the mud and cold. Before, he cleared the ice from the windshield of his motorcar. Put the brown shoebox of photographs on the back seat. Though Dreama wouldn't get inside. Her mind made up to walk. Had me fetch the box and hand it to her, while Jimmy Smart shrugged his shoulders, his gaze bewildered. And that's how I find myself on this road with the collar of my wool coat turned up. Sidestepping here and there because I don't care for the mud myself. Dreama on my left, her purple shawl hiding her hair. While I wonder what we might look like from the sky. The shapes we cut into the ground, that only blackbirds and aeroplanes and God can see. The gloominess inside sits like a stone in my stomach. Reminding me of the pile that are stacked at the foot of my bed. And the truth that Jimmy Smart might leave the field. Go back to his brothers and turn the gallopers in a fortnight's time. When I ask him about it, he tells me nothing's decided. Then distracts me with his pleasing hands. Everywhere at once. When I catch him up, not easy on account of the stride he keeps, I tell him sorry. That he could have stayed in bed where it's warmer. He shrugs. Nods towards St Peter's tower ahead of us, breaking the sky in two. The carrstone looks like rust to me. As if it's made of metal. Dreama slips the shawl from her head, her yellow hair a sudden sunrise. Jimmy Smart gets quiet. And the three of us go to church. Inside, Dreama prefers a pew at the rear, where we can see the whole congregation. Outsiders in our own town. We sit down and listen to the Reverend read. I don't care for his kind of bible talk. By the gaze of Jimmy Smart, neither does he. Though my nose is keen on the scent of faith. This perfumed smell that comes from smooth wood and candles, and musty corners where statues of saints wait patiently. The Reverend recalls the flood that night. A great surge that swept homes and cattle away. And the days afterwards. Lost lives. Those never found. My mother. His voice is weak, though everywhere. Church is clever like that. *And the serpent cast out of his mouth water as a flood after the woman, that he might cause her to be carried away by the flood.* Beside me Dreama stirs. As though the water one year before is whirling around our ankles again. Agitating her. I can't let the water come in. The Wash. This cruel piece of wet I hate in the same way anyone who remembers that night. The sky yellowed beforehand, looming above us. Then she stands up and begins. At first it appears the Reverend doesn't understand. As though she's speaking in tongues. Then louder this time Dreama tells him *Wherefore that field was called, The field of blood, unto this day.* Again and again, until a hundred heads are turned our way.

I'd have walked here sooner to see that, Jimmy Smart says.

Hypocrites—every one of them. Hurling stones
through our windowpanes these past months,
Dreama says.

But why'd you wait till today to tell them? I say.

Couldn't stand it anymore. Been whirling around
my head wondering what to do about it.

Well, you've done it now.

They had it coming. Since the war it's been this
way. Sneering at me and your mother before
the flood took her. Though when they needed
something they couldn't get anywhere else, they
were quick enough to come calling at black
barn. Then—

Go on.

After that night—not one of 'em came.

I know that.

Was like Eliza never even existed. Then those
damned stones started. And now—I'll not go back.

If that's what you want.

It is.

Maybe I should give the stones back? I say.

To the field— Dreama says.

Not before time, Jimmy Smart says.

Dreama is wailing. Turns the two of us around on the road home from church. At once Jimmy Smart quits running off at the mouth about the pile of stones he's a mind to throw back at the field. She's stood in a muddy puddle black as coal. Boots disappeared. Her cheeks wet and worn red with wind, as she gazes on something unseen. The hurt unsettles me. Enough that I want to cover my ears. But I don't. Because I can see what she's remembering. Our field. Though not as it is now, glimmering in the distance. Instead, the morning after the night before. When Dreama had hauled me outdoors at first light. And I'd rubbed my palms across my eyes twice, as a child might. Unable to believe our arrow-shaped field was an island. No matter how I turned, all around my eyes found water. Shiny and everywhere. Dreama stood spellbound by the sight. As if the field itself had somehow held back the wet. While I'd run back into the house and upstairs, pulled open my bedroom window for a better view. Though it made no difference. The dirt was still gone. Hidden beneath the flood. Baffling in the way I couldn't recall where our field ended and another began. Water is mysterious like that. Then I'd seen Dreama turn around and walk towards the edge. Hollering for her to keep out of the water before I'd even made it outside. By now she'd waded waist deep. Her muttering about the distance to town. And as I slipped into the freezing water, disturbing sky reflected there, she'd wanted to know how far I believed the surge had swept. I'd shaken my head. Unable to fathom the truth. Might be the water was all the way in the next county or further. I took Dreama's arm and pulled her back to dry ground. The two of us shaking with cold and effort. Disbelief too. Because no matter how I tried to persuade Dreama about the storm, she wouldn't hear it. Just tugged at her yellow hair that had come undone. Her believing I should have gone after Shane Wright when I'd come home to find my mother absent. Certain she'd find her way home, even without the moon. This truth I wanted to believe. Still mad at her about the oily padlock I'd held in the palm of my hand. Though Dreama was right. We were marooned on account of me. Nothing left to do but wait for the water to retreat. Wait to find my mother, lost out there somewhere in her green dress. And now I watch Jimmy Smart go over to Dreama in three strides, his own boots disturbing the puddle, where he puts his palms against her cheeks. Holds on carefully. Tells her they ought to get home before the cold gets colder. Dreama just moves her head up and down. Mouth ajar. Though no sound comes out. He picks her up, like she's a rare bird, purple and flown from someplace else, and carries her home to the field.

Terrible thing. She'll sleep for the rest of the day I reckon, Jimmy Smart says.

She's getting worse, I say.

What happened at church has worn her out is all.

It's more than that.

How'd you mean?

My mother. She'll not let it go.

Cuz—they never found her?

I guess so.

It's hard for her. On her own and all.

I'm here.

You are. Though I don't suppose it's the same.
Dreama will be better tomorrow morning.
You'll see.

Doubt it.

Cheer up—

My mother—she was selling cigarettes—out at the
old camp, alongside the river. Then the flood went
everywhere.

It's not your fault—

I could have found her. If I hadn't been at Lynn
Boxing Gym with Shane Wright.

You can't know that, Jimmy Smart says.

No—but I feel it, I say.

While Shane Wright had conversed with Bill Bredlau, I'd
leant against the wall and watched the boxing. A pair of
tough young men, around my age, throwing mean punches
beneath yellow lightbulbs. The air thick with sweat and trouble. Their brown leather gloves reminded me of a dead dog
I found once, curled up alongside the field. Where weather
and time had burnished the hide smooth. Being there felt
dangerous. Desire is cunning like that. Then Bill Bredlau
walked on over. Shirt sleeves rolled up. His hair more blue
than black. A Woodbine held between his clever lips. He'd
patted me on my back like I was an animal myself. Said

either of his fighters would gladly spar with me. I'd shaken my head, feeling foolish, because the last thing I'd wanted to do was fight. And Shane Wright slung his arm across my shoulder, as though I were a woman he'd ownership over. Turned me away. As we walked the corridor to the office in back, I wanted to know what Bill Bredlau had meant before. But Shane Wright shrugged and told me to save my curiosity for my notebook. In the office he spoke no more about it. Cleared a space on the wooden desk for me to put my back against, as I took off my trousers and underdrawers. Folded them neatly. Glad there were no windowpanes to hear the storm blow against. As Shane Wright fucked me, the pain something fierce at first, again I thought about Bill Bredlau's words. What they might mean. The wood whined, and all at once the storm found a way inside the room. Where we weren't alone any longer. I'd known it first in Shane Wright's sudden stillness. A disbelief in his eyes where a glint had been before. I turned my head sideways and found Petal stood in the doorway watching us. Behind her Bill Bredlau. Smirking. The whole time I tell Jimmy Smart this tale he is tight lipped. His Woodbine just ash, that would crumble with the smallest breath. His face bleak. A darkness there I'd known before. When a storm whirls inside his head and nowhere else. Even his fist is clenched on the tabletop. As if at any moment I might feel its hardness against my cheek. Though he's not hit me before. And I've no right to believe he might after hearing this. I don't tell him about the things Petal hollered at me in that office. Because he can imagine them for himself. Or what Shane Wright told me on the drive home about Bill Bredlau. Wind rocking the motor-car. The storm coming from everywhere at once. Even the road beneath the wheels. Me not having any concern about my mother or anything other than the heat in my backside reminding me of what I am. Quietly Jimmy Smart gets up. Walks into the hallway, and goes upstairs. I sit still at the table. Unsure what to do. I feel an urge to go out to black barn. Gather a shovel and break apart the frozen dirt in our field. Above the bomb. Because I believe Jimmy Smart is in my room this minute gathering his belongings to leave here. Return to his brothers to turn the gallopers. Those wooden horses he promised me a ride upon. When Jimmy Smart comes back into the kitchen, his hands are heavy with the stones from the foot of my bed.

Where're you going? I say.

To do what we should have done an age ago. Throw these damn stones back in the field. Cuz that's where they belong, Jimmy Smart says.

You're not mad at me?

I'm not.

That's good—

Though I don't want you going near Bill Bredlau again. Or that damn gym.

But—

Nothing but trouble.

I promised Shane Wright.

Then break it.

I can't do that.

Don't see why Shane Wright'd want to see Bill Bredlau anyway.

Forget about it—

Here—take some of these stones.

I'm no use at throwing—never have been, I say.

Then today's as good a day as any to learn, Jimmy Smart says.

The wind doesn't care which way it blows. Wind is wild like that. I pedal my pushbike harder along Marsh Road, on the way to Lynn. Wishing my wool coat would beat back the bitter morning. This same cold that conspired with the mud on the road to church yesterday. Though I won't think on the service. What Dreama did. Her hatred towards the congregation let loose like a wildfire. Something fierce. Or what came afterwards with the pile of stones that are gone from the foot of my bed. Because it's over. Like the photographs Dreama left in church on a smooth pew. And now I want the troubles with Adie Lovekin to go the same way. Why I set off at dawn to see Bill Bredlau. To ask him if he'll talk some sense into Shane Wright. Even if Jimmy Smart is hopping mad about it. Believing I ought to keep clear of Lynn Boxing Gym. Him telling me as much while he'd pulled on his white underdrawers first thing. Above the sky is a similar colour. Empty, the birds all blown away. Between here and North Lynn docks in the distance, the fields are dead after the flood-water. Even one year on. As if this place has forgotten itself. And I am baffled that dirt can stand still while everything else about me whirls around and around. Now Jimmy Smart is considering his situation. With the Mart coming to Lynn in a fortnight, and his brothers wanting him back with the showpeople instead of hiring a new hand. The three of them turning the horses that leap and snort and gallop. The thought of him leaving the field makes me ache something fierce. Reminding me of the black water that surrounded me and Dreama that night. Soaking us with terror. This whirling inside my head takes me past cranes hauling heavy loads and pavements waking up. Until I'm outside Lynn Boxing Gym. Lean my pushbike against the brick wall, where an old man tells me I'm too early. I nod because I know this already. Walk around back to bang against another door that has brown paint peeling. I stand and wait. Until I can hear someone on the other side. When the door opens I step back a pace. Bill Bredlau gazes with a familiarity that unsettles me. Because he knows what I look like without my underdrawers. Same way Shane Wright does. They both have smooth hair too, more blue than black. Greased in place with clever wax that smells like soap and leather. Behind him, a bare bulb rocks back and forth. Then he motions me to come inside. Closes the door behind. I follow down a narrow corridor and into his office. There's no window in here, and all at once I wonder if Shane Wright has a piece of sky he can gaze at above the Heath. If it wasn't for my desire to help him, I wouldn't be standing here in this room again. Bill Bredlau sits down behind the wooden desk, busy with loose paper and film canisters. Lights a cigarette. It occurs to me I haven't taken off my wool gloves. Or uttered a word.

You're a sight. Not laid eyes on you since— Bill Bredlau says.

Day of the flood, I say.

That's right.

I'm here 'bout—Shane Wright.

Figured as much. How's he doing?

Not good. You've not—written back to him.

What's it to you?

He wants you to visit him.

Bet he does. Though I've no desire to go to prison.

He told me—'bout the two of you.

Is that so?

It is. Can't you convince him—to tell the truth?

And why would I do that?

Then he'd be free of the trouble.

But he wouldn't.

How'd you mean?

Here— Take a look.

What's this? I say.

Your Shane Wright, Bill Bredlau says.

I believe my yellow hair has caused me more misfortune than not. Jimmy Smart told me so after he moved into black barn. When the moon was full and tasted of nothing. That it was the first thing to catch his eye. Then later on that the colour reminded him of his lions Ezzah and Afreen. I've never seen a lion, except in a picture book. So when he nuzzles me in the place between my dick and arsehole, claiming I smell like a lion here too, I won't believe him. He is trying to mend my mood. Though I don't see that anything, especially concerning my dick, will make me feel better now Dreama's disappeared. Jimmy Smart tells me it's a predicament for sure. Her note giving nothing away. Words can be maddening like that. I get up and pull on my underdrawers. Trousers too. Jimmy Smart sighs. Leans back against the headboard and lights a Woodbine. Outside the window is black. We haven't eaten and my stomach growls. In truth I've not been myself since the morning with Bill Bredlau at Lynn Boxing Gym. Him sliding a handful of photographs across the desk. Where I saw Shane Wright stark naked. Sometimes by himself. His skin pale and shiny with oil. Dick hard. Then one with him pushed up against another man. Who looked back over his shoulder, and might have been the boxer from the night of the flood. Another even more wild. With a different man I've no name for. I'd known my face had gone another colour. My underdrawers so easily disturbed. It was hard to fathom that Shane Wright had allowed Bill Bredlau to take these photographs. Him believing they'd make him something in America he couldn't be here. Those muscle magazines are dangerous like that. I've said nothing to Jimmy Smart about the photographs. Because he'll likely kill him. For what he wants from me. And that wouldn't do any one of us no good. Then he tells me he's hungry too. Downstairs, I heat up stew leftover from the night before, while the showman cuts chunks of bread haphazardly.

You know, that's the first time I've seen you smile all day, Jimmy Smart says.

Not been here for most of it, I say.

Still a smartarse.

I guess.

We'll find Dreama. Cuz she can't have gone too far.

We?

I'm not going anywhere. My brothers will have to manage without me. They have before now.

What 'bout Esme?

I'll take tomorrow off. Go see her. My brothers too.

And what if they won't hear you?

They will. Enough now. You ever gonna tell me what happened at the gym with Bill Bredlau? Will he go see Shane Wright in prison?

He won't.

That doesn't surprise me.

'Bout tomorrow.

What of it?

Can I go with you?

Best you don't.

Because of the way I am? I say.

Just cuz it's something I have to do by myself is all,
Jimmy Smart says.

The yard is not the same without Shane Wright. Even
though I've had days and days since summer to get used
to the red brick walls without him here. Since they said he
took Adie Lovekin and her voice. Might be it smells another
way too. Same way dirt smells different in summer than
winter. On account of the pleasing bacteria buried beneath.
I miss his scent of soap and leather. His inky hand holding a
Woodbine. Metallic smoke everywhere. Coloured like the
sky above me getting ready to rain. Mac Sam has been on
my back since hiring Ray Turner to run the Heidelberg.
Convinced Shane Wright is gone for good. They could be
brothers with the way they mirror one another. Though
Ray Turner is wider and Mac Sam taller. Both gaze at me
with suspicious eyes. Even more so when I open my sissy
mouth to answer one of them. Though I wonder why
they bother because everything I utter appears to make
their ears ache. Their foreheads frown. Yesterday, when I
returned late from North End, Mac Sam wanted to know
where I'd been. I told him to visit the men out at the old
POW camp, in case they'd seen Dreama. Or heard of her
whereabouts. That I'd make up the time at the end of the
day. He'd grunted. As if I cursed or something worse. After

Dreama's outburst in church Sunday past, the townies hate us even more than the prisoners who never went home after the war. Mac Sam told me then that selling cigarettes was how my mother ended up in such misfortune. That he wouldn't be surprised if Dreama went the same way down by the river. Like both of them had it coming. Jimmy Smart is right, townies are ignorant. Now Mac Sam's in the yard hounding me, on his way to use the privy at the far end behind a blue door. The buttons of his trousers already unfastened. He turns back and shakes his head at the sight of me standing idle. Hands stuffed in pockets to keep the cold from settling across my knuckles, turning them blue. I listen to him piss. All of a sudden I can picture Dreama drifting through the moody water. On her way to Blackguard Sand. Whirling with hundreds of pairs of mismatched shoes turning around and around in the wet. And china cups that are so fine they float amongst the jellyfish. Then Mac Sam is finished relieving himself. His lips making movements I can't hear, not two inches from the tip of my nose. His breath stinks of Woodbines and old tea. Louder he tells me Ray Turner needs me to help shift more paper. I nod. My arms still ache from before. As if they no longer feel attached to my shoulders. Mac Sam keeps on at me. Calling me boy. Yet I'm unable to convince my boots to turn around and head inside the printshop. To be restless and standing still, baffles me. I wish Jimmy Smart were here. I can't stand not knowing where he is. Dreama too. Both missing for three days now. Then what little light had hung in the sky overhead disappears, and it begins to rain.

You listening to me boy? Mac Sam says.

I am, I say.

That paper won't shift itself.

Guess not.

Then get to it boy.

Don't—call me that.

Suspect you're right. I apologise. Seems to me *girl* would be more fitting.

Dreama—was right 'bout you.

How's that?

You're a—hypocrite. Way you and the townies look down on Dreama. And my mother before the flood.

Is that so?

It is. Didn't stop your wife coming out to our field. When she needed something she couldn't get nowhere else. Then—we were good enough.

Leave my wife out of this. I ought to fire you.

You can't do that.

Why not?

I'm quitting—

Good. And don't come back here. You little sissy, Mac Sam says.

I'd sooner burn in hell, I say.

Rain beneath the platform roof sounds sombre. Like a hymn from church that Dreama would hum sometimes before the flood, while mending the hem of her dress. I'd never cared for it, and now all at once I would gladly have her here. The sound filling my ears. Her yellow hair a sudden brightness, while she smokes a Woodbine. My insides are whirling still after the printshop with Mac Sam. And now, if things weren't bad enough already, I am without work. Stood at Wolferton station, where the platform has a scatter of old men waiting for the Lynn train, and a pretty woman clutching her heavy coat about the neck. There's no sign of Jimmy Smart in his blue porter's cap. Hope is fragile like that. So easily gone, it reminds me I behave like a boy sometimes. Yet I'll never have to hear Mac Sam call me such again. I lean my pushbike against the brick wall and brace myself for the ticket office. As I know Petal will be there, behind the glass. When I step inside, the clock above the arch strikes two. Dreama would say this means something. The steel blue hands foretelling a truth of sorts. I don't know about that. Petal looks up and sees me gazing at her. There's no way to know what she's wondering. She turns away, slips out of view, until the glass is more like a mirror I can see myself in. Hair wet and a different colour. Like wet sand. Eyes that appear bruised and troubled. As though I've been in the ring with one of Bill Bredlau's fighters for five rounds. Then Petal is beside me. Telling me if I want to talk it had better be quick. I follow behind until we are outside behind the station house. Last time I'd stood here was the day Jimmy Smart took a pickaxe to the dirt, while I'd followed behind with a shovel. When afterwards we went to the riverbank and he turned my world sideways. Now the ground is healed. As if we had disturbed nothing. I'm aching to ask Petal if she's had any word from the showman. This must be what pride feels like, unable to open my mouth and say the words. Instead, I tell her the truth about Bill Bredlau. Even if she won't want to hear a word of it. Because I am worn tired from everything unsaid since the night of the flood. When she had found me and Shane Wright in Lynn Boxing Gym office. I tell her too of going to see Bill Bredlau at the start of the week. Because Shane Wright had wanted me to. And I'd believed somehow he might talk some sense into him about the troubles that are Adie Lovekin. That he shouldn't be behind bars for something he didn't do. I hesitate. Unsure at first whether or not to tell her what Bill Bredlau asked from me in return for his help. Photographs, and more. All the while she smokes her Woodbine. Plays with a piece of hair that won't stay in place no matter how she tucks it away. Reminds me of how things were the summer before the flood. The two of us with our backs against the field. Dizzy with the scent of growing grass, and smoking too many Woodbines. My limbs getting longer in the heat, and she more beautiful. I'd told her my plan to pack a suitcase and go someplace else. Someplace shiny. Where people might not mind my sissy-sounding voice. Where I could write down all the words I believed lived inside my head. Now I know where words really come from on account of Jimmy Smart. Hitchhiking on my breath. And all at once I'm finished with my concern for Petal. Tired of being sorry. Because I am not the man who wronged her.

Your concern can find someplace else to rest,
Petal says.

If that's what you want, I say.

Those photographs—aren't real. You're a liar.

Believe what you want. But—I've seen 'em. Shane
Wright. And other lads from the gym. All of 'em
bare-arsed. And I want no part of it.

He wouldn't do a thing like that.

Yet—the day of the storm, he brought you right
to us.

He's not like you and Shane Wright— Bill Bredlau
wants to marry me.

Why'd you want to go and marry—a man like that?
When—you know the truth 'bout him.

You don't understand.

It's true—I don't.

I want him.

Then I'm sorry for you Petal.

You? Sorry for me. You're the fool. Running
around after Jimmy Smart like a girl. As though the
two of you aren't perverts, Petal says.

You and Bill Bredlau—deserve each other, I say.

At first I believe the yellow light could be Jimmy Smart come home. His motorcar moving down our track, until it comes to a standstill ten feet ahead. Engine ticking. I'm outside with my arms folded across my chest to keep the cold out, because in eagerness I didn't think to collect my coat on the way here. The brightness is like looking at two sunrises happening at once. Before, I'd come home to find the house silent. A melancholy stillness that made me wake a fire hastily. My hair soaked with rain. Trousers too. That I hung on the back of a chair to dry off while I'd peeled potatoes. Seemed even my insides were wet with the terrible day. I set about making a stew to calm my mind, that whirled around and around like one of Jimmy Smart's rides. Always returning to where I was. Wrong to believe the chores might make me feel better somehow. Jimmy Smart would say I'm distracting myself. And I'd tell him he's right, if it were he who climbs out of the motorcar. Instead, Bill Bredlau walks towards me. Like a bull in his dark wool coat. I consider what it means, him being here at this hour. Nothing good I suspect. When he speaks, his breath is everywhere at once, on account of the headlights reaching across the cold night. Though I've no desire, I invite him to come inside. Before I catch a fierce cold myself. Inside, he pulls out a chair and sits down at the table. Lights a Woodbine while he settles himself. I push my hands deep into my trouser pockets and gaze on him. In lamp light his hair is still blue, and shiny as boot polish. I can even smell the pomade. The scent of musk, and something else I don't know the name of. But it's pleasing. Citrus, from somewhere warm. Bill Bredlau is troubled. I see it only now his eyes are searching my own. And he tells me Shane Wright is dead. That he's hanging in a cell at the prison on Mousehold Heath. He says it plainly. Nothing to smooth the edge. I open my mouth to tell him he's wrong. That he's talking in tongues. Though no words come out. Nothing hitchhiking on my breath. Truth is troublesome like that. I don't know how I feel this so surely. Yet I do. As if I've known Shane Wright was dead since sunrise. Since the day they put him behind bars for taking Adie Lovekin. Though I still can't let myself believe what I don't want to about these troubles. About the man who took her voice. Even now. I sit down across from Bill Bredlau. Not because I feel faint. He slides his pack of cigarettes across the pine tabletop. I light one. In my head I hear Shane Wright swing back and forth like Dreama's pendulum. Creaking. His trousers wet through with piss. Skin bluer than any blue I've ever seen before.

Shane Wright had me down as his next of kin, Bill Bredlau says.

His brother died—in the desert, I say.

They'll be reunited then.

Why'd you even come here?

He'd have wanted me to tell you.

And now you have—

Was always gonna end this way. Shane Wright was broken.

You're wrong.

No— And you know it. Even if you won't listen. He didn't have a chance. Was never gonna make it to America with that big dream of his. Men like him never do—

He could've, if it weren't for those pictures— You ruined him.

Never once heard him complain about 'em. The truth is, he wanted to be something he wasn't. Taking Adie Lovekin wasn't ever going to change him.

You don't know he took her.

Suppose I don't. But my guess is, you believe it too, Bill Bredlau says.

I believe—you broke him, I say.

The field wants me. As it has time and again. I was seven years old when the dirt first called. After the Blitz. On a morning unlike any I'd known. Sky more yellow than blue and all around us. We'd all been woken by the noise in the night. A bomb falling whistles like a kettle on the boil. I'd wondered if a German bomb falls differently than one of our own. Makes another noise. Though reaching back I remember the hole more than anything else. Ten feet wide. The bomb unexploded in the bottom unlike anything I'd ever laid eyes on. Conjured from another place in-between earth and sky. For the longest while the three of us did nothing but gaze. Dreama and my mother smoking their Woodbines in wonder. Afterwards, nobody told. I'd sat cross-legged nearby while my mother and Dreama filled in the hole with a shovel each. Resentful not to have one for myself. I'd wanted to help. Though they wouldn't hear of it. Then in time, like a sickness of sorts, we all wound up out there on that piece of ground where the grass doesn't care to grow. One after the other. As though there was a length of string tying the four of us together. A curse is persuasive like that. First Dreama turning in circles. Then my mother, who'd put her back against the dirt above the bomb. Sometimes I'd find her writing one of her long letters on paper scented with violets. Sometimes, she'd read them to me. Though I'd not understand their meaning. Even if the sound had pleased my ears. Dreama told me once my mother's letters weren't really real. I'd creep outside in the night, damp with sweat and too restless to sleep, and wonder what she'd meant by that. Beneath a moon that seemed to pull something out of me, as it might shift the tides. This thing that makes me something other than I appear to be. And here I am now, with a shovel of my own. Introducing the steel edge to the hard ground beneath me. Again and again. I've been at it since sunrise. Unconcerned with the cold that's cracked my knuckles open. Reckon a pickaxe would be better. Its bite meaner. Though I failed to find one in black barn, just this here shovel and the sight of Jimmy Smart's fold-out bed. A blue blanket rolled at the foot. My mood dark as the dirt piled all about me. I'm mad at Shane Wright for taking Adie Lovekin. Because I believe he did. Mad because he was a coward. And yet I want to hold him. A blackbird swoops past. A sudden blur from the corner of my eye. Then three more. Reminding me of the disappeared. Though I keep on digging while rain comes again, moving me along. When I look up the showman is there. He has a week's worth of beard, and a blue bruise on his forehead shaped like an arrow. His gaze lit, then gloomy.

Hey stranger, Jimmy Smart says.

Is it really you? I say.

Who else? What in the hell you doing? Cuz you're scaring me.

Digging.

I can see that. I ain't blind Eli. Why you out here? It's freezing.

Won't be when I'm done here.

Come on. Put the shovel down.

No.

I'm not fooling.

Why'd you stay away? Without a word.

I telephoned the station to let them know. I figured you'd go there when I didn't come back. Things were harder than I thought they'd be. My brothers ain't happy. None of my people are.

You gone. And Dreama. Now Shane Wright.

How'd you mean Shane Wright?

He's hanging out at the Heath.

Hanging?

Killed himself yesterday morning.

I can't believe that. Come on inside now.

I'm all right here.

I wasn't asking.

You know—I reckon Dreama's dead too, I say.

Your Dreama's not dead. She's with Esme and my brothers, Jimmy Smart says.

The wet won't quit. It's been pouring down since Jimmy Smart came home yesterday. Since he took hold of the shovel and banged it into the ground, where it stood like a scarecrow guarding the hole I'd dug. Then he'd taken me inside the house, his palms against my back moving me upstairs, and put me to bed after carefully pulling off my damp clothes. The whole while I had nothing to say. Not even about his arrow-shaped bruise. As if the very sight of him had left me struck dumb. After he laid an extra wool blanket atop the bed, I'd slept clear though until now, where I'm stood at the backdoor watching the field. It's too far away to know what's happened to my hole. The rain a wall between here and there. Though I have a suspicion the showman returned to the dirt after he laid me down. Put right my wrong. Until the ground is level once more with his effort. I smoke my Woodbine. There's comfort in the knowledge Dreama is somewhere safe. Even if I don't yet know the circumstances. Seems hard to believe Sunday past we were on the road to church. The showman striding ahead while Dreama clutched her found photographs that belong to the farmers and their wives. I wonder if the Reverend will preach about the relentless rain in church this day. Tell his congregation of Noah and his Ark. Then Jimmy Smart is behind me, turning me around. Eyes wide and serious, as if he's undecided how hard to kiss me. His breath smells of sleep and doubt. Instead, he moves past me to where his boots are laid. Tucks loose laces inside to save tying them. Goes outside to use the privy, pushing the backdoor shut behind him. The kitchen is quiet without the rain. While he's gone I feed the stove with enough coal to drive out the cold and damp. Fill the kettle to make tea. The bread is stale, but I work to cut the worst of it away. Place two slices each on the tabletop. When Jimmy Smart comes back inside I ask him if he wants scrambled eggs. He nods. Sits down at the pine table and lights a Woodbine. Watches me closely. There's a world of questions whirling around my head I've a mind to ask him. And I won't wait any longer. All of a sudden there's the surprising sound of glass breaking, and I know a stone has been hurled through a bedroom windowpane. Likely Dreama's. At once Jimmy Smart is back in his boots and through the door. After tying my laces, I'm following behind. Down the track and out on to the road, where the showman is gaining on two dark pushbikes. He hauls the nearest clean off the road, tumbling into the hedge. Still brown with winter and the flood. While the other rides away, Jimmy Smart keeps hold of this boy. Alongside us, the pushbike lies in a muddy puddle. Wheel still turning. By the look of him he can't be much more than twelve years old. His gaze wild and everywhere. As if the showman might murder him. Over and over he wants to know why he's hurled these stones. Shakes him so hard I wonder if his backbone will snap any moment. Hurting my ears with its crack. The boy is crying now and Jimmy Smart stills himself. Grows quiet. The rain keeps coming. He lets go. Rights the boy's pushbike and offers up the handlebars. Hurriedly the boy climbs on and pedals away. Zigzagging down the road like a broken blackbird. We stand and stare. Our underdrawers soaked clear. Vests too. Back at the house we strip off. Jimmy Smart collects two blankets from upstairs. Tells me he'll clear away the broken glass later. With a chair each we wrap ourselves in itchy wool, together in front of the stove.

You feeling like yourself again? Cuz you've more colour than yesterday, Jimmy Smart says.

Running in the rain'll do that, I say.

Suppose it will. Little bastard—

I'm glad you let him go.

He was just a boy. They'll be scared now. Doubt we'll see 'em again.

You'll tell me 'bout Dreama now?

I'll get to your Dreama. But first, Shane Wright. How'd you hear?

Bill Bredlau drove out here after the prison called him.

Is that so?

He reckons Shane Wright took Adie Lovekin.

If he's right, then he got what he deserved. You believe it too?

155

I believe Shane Wright, somewhere inside, was *wrong*.

Jesus. Don't see how we'll ever know for sure.

I can't think on Shane Wright any more today.

Understood—

My Dreama?

Could hardly believe my eyes to find Dreama and Esme are together. Both of 'em shacked up in her caravan like two peas in a pod. I'd known Dreama was hellbent on introducing herself to Esme and the showpeople, her being fascinated with that pendulum and all. But I'd no clue she'd go and find them herself.

When is she coming back?

She's safe is what matters. I've no desire to be back there. Got this here bruise for my trouble.

But I want to see her, I say.

Thing is, she doesn't want to see you, Jimmy Smart says.

My sissy-sounding voice brings me more misfortune than not. It occurs to me this might be why Dreama has no desire to be around. These troubles I collect like stones, before we threw them back in the field. He tells me I'm wrong to worry. That she'll come around in time. Her indifference is on account of the flood one year on. Water running from there to here. And what happened in church the week past with the Reverend. Yet I do worry. Whether or not I'll ever gaze on her again. After the flood Dreama told me my mother was the only woman who ever understood her. Insides and out. She'd sat at the kitchen table smoking her woodbine, holding a photograph of them together. Two sisters with yellow hair, both beautiful, and no man around to remind them so. I wonder if it's the same way with her and Esme now. If she's found something akin to another family, in a new place. Two peas in a pod Jimmy Smart had said. My Dreama alongside Esme, who reads the cards for the townswomen who want to know everything they shouldn't. When I suggest this to the showman he reminds me without any meanness that I'm behaving foolishly. That Dreama has been gone for one week. Unfolds his arms. Drinks the last of his tea from a delicate china cup. His heavy hand at odds with the pretty painted violets. Enquires quietly if I've made up my mind to visit Mousehold Heath today. Though Shane Wright's body will have been moved to a mortuary, the prison itself is where the last trace of him will linger I reckon. Jimmy Smart believes returning here one last time will put an end to everything. Bury the past. I don't know if endings behave this way. If anything is ever really done. Least not until there's no one left breathing who remembers. Memory is mysterious like that. As peculiar as the mind that make these instances return again and again to haunt us. And when Jimmy Smart leans across the tabletop to nudge my arm, I put down the pencil. Close my notebook. Tell him he's right about going to prison. Though in part I believe he's trying to outrun the rain, still coming down heavy. Him anticipating a different kind of weather across county. In his motorcar, the road more like a river running, I listen to him talk about the Smart Brothers. Where he tells me being the youngest is hard work. Same way digging holes in dirt is. Even worse with them being twins, sharing something unique between themselves. After his old man Bullet died, the three of them inherited the gallopers, and for a time Jimmy Smart navigated his world with the belief he belonged there. That with Bullet buried he could put the past with Ezzah and Afreen behind him. These lions he loved. Though soon afterwards he got called up for National Service. I ask him whereabouts. A place unlike anywhere else called the Suez Canal. I want to know what that means, and he tells me some places are unique in a way that can change a person. When he came back two years later he was something other than before. Seems to me we have something else in common. Something unseen between the two of us. More than being twins. Then Jimmy Smart points to his forehead. The arrow-shaped bruise is a shade of purple now, same as Dreama's knitted shawl.

They'll never understand. Me wanting something other than that life. Cuz they're ignorant like the townies. Don't matter how hard they hit me, I'll not be like them, Jimmy Smart says.

What is it you're wanting? I say.

You promise not to laugh? It's pretty wild.

I do.

I wanna farm your field.

What 'bout the curse?

We both know what's buried beneath the dirt. It can stay there.

Been wondering.

Go on—

All these troubles of late with Shane Wright and Dreama. The stones too.

What about 'em?

Might be my fault. On account of me being the way I am.

How'd you mean?

Sometimes I wonder what my voice would sound like—if I wasn't this way inclined.

Why's anything the way it is? Some things just are.

Doubt Shane Wright saw it that way.

He was disturbed. Nothing to be done about it.

You reckon it will be different for us?

There's a chance.

This really what you want? I say.

Rain's wearing on me something terrible, Jimmy Smart says.

Jimmy Smart is stark naked in lamp light. Could spend the rest of my days familiarising myself with each part of him from toes to crown. The shape of him is something else. How two different men can share the same skin and have it hung about their bones in such a way as to make one beautiful and the other nothing much at all, is a mystery to me. There's no part of him that's bashful. Even his gaze. Taunting me. The evening before we'd moved my mother's gramophone upstairs and stood it in the corner alongside the bedroom window. Since, Jimmy Smart has been playing records to drown out the rain running down our window-panes. Though not like he is now. Drunk on Esme's herbal bottle he's been tipping back since midday. The air thick with blue smoke and sweat. His dick restless, pointing more up than down, while he turns in circles dancing around and around as the floorboards murmur. And again, it appears there's a fire burning beneath his skin. Like it had during the bonfire behind the station that night with Petal. He tells me these vices will be his downfall eventually. Though I'm not sure if he means the alcohol, dancing without any clothes, or me. Might be all three of us. A holy trinity of sorts. Yet I like it when he drinks too much because everything slows down and he's loose with words in a way he isn't ordinarily. Proclaiming sweet things that make my cheeks hot. My ears ache for more. The disturbance in my underdrawers pitched as a tent might be. Then he reaches for the silver tin of balm laid beside the jug. Unscrews the lid slowly. Takes a big glob and rubs it against his own backside. My mouth must be ajar, as he begins laughing like he knows something I've yet to understand. Another one of his distractions. Then matter-of-factly he says I can fuck him if I like. Though he'll not make a habit of it. I tug down my underdrawers too quickly and my dick slaps my belly, encouraging his smile. He passes me the tin and I grease myself up. Wondering how exactly I should begin because I have never fucked no one before. My dick's so hard it hurts. I go slowly. How the showman does. Not like Shane Wright, who was never careful. This feels like nothing I've known before. Making me dizzy until the sensation sends pictures fluttering across my eyelids I didn't know I'd seen before. There's a full moon that's really a shiny coin in the palm of a strong man's hand. When he flips the coin it spins too slowly like the air is suddenly solid, and lands heads up on the dirt, Shane Wright's face gazing up at me. And I'm back at the Heath where Jimmy Smart parked his motorcar two days before, everything stained blue. Even the grass bending towards the brick walls that dark clouds grazed. The rain lighter, as if it had tired of falling. Jimmy Smart stood behind, leaving me to say farewell to the ghost of Shane Wright. Because words had no desire to hitchhike on my breath, I'd raised my hand and waved. Feeling foolish until the showman nodded his approval. Seems to me some goodbyes are better left unspoken. I open my eyes. Jimmy Smart's back is glimmering with sweat. I'm bucked up against him, head back, roaring like one of his lions, unable to hear the sound of my own sissy voice.

What's it like, being with a woman? I say.

Don't ask foolish things, Jimmy Smart says.

I want to know.

Why's it matter to you?

Matters how you see me. Sometimes I wonder if you think of me more like a woman. On account of the way I talk and all.

You're being an idiot.

Might be the case. But I'm not a woman.

I know that. Even if you've pretty skin. Truth is, I ain't ever slept with a woman. Nor have I any desire to.

That the truth?

Every last bit of it.

I was thinking.

And what might that be?

'Bout the gallopers, I say.

Soon. I promise, Jimmy Smart says.

The Mart is making ready for All Saint's five days from now. There's long wooden stalls being built where townies can hurl coconuts beneath canvas. And steam engines chucking smoke everywhere making ready to turn rides on the marketplace. Now it's quit raining, the Big Wheel appears like a cog in the sky, moving dark clouds onwards. I ask a woman with wild hair if she can tell me where Esme is. She tips her head sideways. Tells me Esme doesn't sound like any name she's heard of, believing me to be trouble. Then I try enquiring about Dreama. That she's my aunt.

Now she glares. Worse than before. And puts her back to me, busying herself. Seems to me she has the same manner as Jimmy Smart. Each time I asked him when I could go see Dreama all he uttered was soon, until my ears couldn't hardly stand hearing it. After he climbed into his motorcar this morning, reluctant to return to the station and Peg, I'd dressed hurriedly. Collected my pushbike from black barn and set off for town, pedalling alongside barren fields while considering rainy days with the showman. Two of us hiding out at the house. Barely bothering with our clothes, even though it's bone cold still, because our hands were busy being everywhere. Him turning me around and bucking up against my backside. Slick with his new tin of balm to ease the pain. Until I'm dizzy with desire. And now I find myself asking a man my own age if he's seen Jimmy Smart. Because I'll not mention Dreama again around here. He tells me the Smart Brothers are readying their gallopers at the centre of the market square. A hard-earned pitch. I nod as if he's telling me something I know already. Ask after Esme. Reckons she's likely on the other side of Lynn. Where the showpeople overwinter at Knights Hill. I have a desire to go see the gallopers. Run my palm against the wooden horses. Search out the grey one. Instead, I get back on my pushbike and ride away, wondering what awaits me.

You're—not easy to find, I say.

This Eliza's boy? Esme says.

The same, Dreama says.

Suppose it has to be with that head of yellow hair.
I'll leave the two of you be.

I knew you'd come.

What are you doing here? What's wrong with—me
and the field all of a sudden?

Who said anything's wrong?

Jimmy Smart told me you've no desire to be around
me—for the time being.

Don't know where he's gathered that idea from.
Because it isn't true.

You saying Jimmy Smart is a liar?

Sometimes you're exactly like your mother.

How'd you mean?

Coming all this way to tell me off. Like I'm a child.
Might not occur to you that I've been taking care of
myself since way before you were born.

Where's—all this come from? Is it me? The
way I am?

Now you're being foolish. You ever heard me utter
one bad word about it?

I haven't.

There's your proof then. This has nothing to do
with you.

I don't understand—

Then quit trying to.

What would you have me do? I say.

Come meet Esme, Dreama says.

Day I turned seven years old my mother told me she'd called me Eli on account of its similarity to her own name, Eliza. That she wanted me to be just like her. Even though I am a boy. Later, she believed this explained my peculiar manner, same way I'd inherited her yellow hair. I'd been born with a fondness for pretty things, keeping my fingernails clean, hair combed. And a desire to gaze at men in a way that would bring me more misfortune than not. Alongside my mother in the field, grass alive with wild things, shimmering in sun-light, she taught me about men. How she'd no need to have one around the place. Men, she believed, would eventually do their damnedest to disappear her. Dreama too. Men are wilful like that. And I wonder if that's where my will went that afternoon in our field, soaring off on the back of a clever blackbird. Me believing something about myself that someone else pushed inside my head. Where it's stayed stuck since. Even if she hadn't meant me any harm. That's how I find myself sat opposite Dreama and Esme in her caravan, before a scatter of worn cards on the tabletop telling me if I'm fortunate or not. There's a dark tower struck by bright lightning, with people tumbling down. Beside this, The Fool. Making me uneasy because the stirring in my stomach warns it was foolish to have come here today without telling Jimmy Smart beforehand. Who resembles the beggar on the card now he has an unruly beard after the rain. All the while Dreama gazes on. She seems at home here in a way I've not known her to behave since before the flood. This hurts. But I brush it away. Gaze about. All around me the caravan is filled with strange things I don't rightly know the name of. Colourful cloth hung about everywhere, that glimmers behind a shelf filled with glass jars. Inside are the herbs I reckon she used to conjure Jimmy Smart's special bottle of alcohol. Then Esme turns over another card with a woman who has yellow hair, called The Empress. This card appears upside-down and she dismisses it with a sudden wave. Tells me the cards are misbehaving. If she says so. And we head outside into winter light that threatens to be a similar shade of yellow as the day of the flood. Though Dreama doesn't mention this. No words out of her mouth about how it must mean something. A sign of sorts. Instead, she links her arm through my own and we wander towards the far side of this field, where a line of tall trees stand guard. Beneath, a trailer that's been in the long grass for years by my measure. The paint on the boards above the cage has faded away, until there's nothing left that means anything. There's no way to know for sure if this is Jimmy Smart's cage. The very same that held Ezzah and Afreen. Yet I want to believe it might be. I reach out and take hold of the bars. Pull myself forward until my nose is filled with different scents. Rust and urine. Earth. And something similar to camphor. If Dreama weren't beside me I'd climb up to the roof of the cage and put my back against the wood there. Close my eyes tightly and see if I can hear Jimmy Smart roaring with lions. These wild beasts pacing back and forth. The three of them sharing the same restlessness inside. An ache to be somewhere else. Dreama leans in, her breath smells of violets, and she tells me the lions are buried beyond the trees.

How'd you know about Jimmy Smart's lions? I say.

Esme— She's like a mother to him, Dreama says.

And what is she to you?

Don't see that it's any of your concern.

Is when you're out here instead of at home beside
the field.

That damn field. Some days I don't care if I ever lay
eyes on it again.

You don't mean that.

Yet I do.

Can't see how you'd rather be here. Somewhere
they shoot lions dead.

Been ten years since.

That's not so long. When are you coming home?

Esme says I have a gift.

More riddles. You mean Adie Lovekin's pendulum?

The same.

She's fooling with you.

And why would she go and do that?

Who knows—

Don't holler at me— It's been one year since Eliza.
And this is the first piece of joy I've known.

Doesn't make any sense, I say.

Don't see that it has to, Dreama says.

Even his leather boots sound livid. Pacing back and forth across the ground outside Esme's caravan. Wild-eyed Jimmy Smart is madder than I've known him before, going off at the mouth about my being here without his saying so. That I've broken the rules. His breath blue in the cold air. Behind his head Dreama and Esme appear as puppets in the window, their silhouettes like something from another place. And when I push my hands into my coat pockets, tell him I'd not needed his permission to search out Dreama, or care any longer for his stupid rules, he stops still. Gazes at me for the longest while. Takes out his pack of Woodbines and lights two. Passes me the spare. His shoulders slacken and he leans back onto the caravan with a slow sigh. Above, the light that appeared yellow before has gone from the sky. Dusk threatens, heavy and sombre, its shadows already pooling all about us. Jimmy Smart talks quietly. Tells me all day long he had a hunch I'd go looking for Dreama first chance I got. That he should have known better than to leave me alone. Him believing me fragile after Shane Wright hung himself out at Mousehold Heath. Worried even, I'd dig up the dirt again to get at what's buried beneath. Our bomb. Why we never told a soul. More than once in the past days he's wanted to know what pulls me out to the middle of the field more often than not. Dreama too. And my mother before the flood. Truth can be puzzling like that. At first I'd believed it was to keep the townies away from black barn and the goods they sold in secret. Because I was too young to understand. Now I know it's something else. Something akin to survival. My mother and Dreama understanding that sooner or later they'd get rubbed out even before they disappear. And to be reminded somehow made them more alive, walking barefoot about this truth. Yet I'd wanted to find a truth of my own. Even packed my suitcase, hellbent on leaving. Because my mother disappeared anyway. Then on a sweltering afternoon Jimmy Smart blew in like a whirlwind of sorts. Full of illusions, stirring everything up. A man more alive than any I'd ever gazed upon. I open my mouth to let out some of what's on my mind. No matter how foolish it might be. To tell him that thing a man mustn't say to another man. Though I'm interrupted. There's two gleaming lights casting their glare, turning the showman around with an urgency that unsettles me. The motorcar comes to a stop and two men climb out, leaving the yellow lit. The Smart Brothers come striding across the way. I glance at Jimmy Smart, his face every emotion stirred together until I've no chance of untangling which is closest to the surface, colouring his skin. All at once the twins circle me like I'm prey and might taste pleasing. Even Dreama appears troubled. She's stood at the caravan door, Esme has hold of her arm. Then the twins take hold of Jimmy Smart and haul him away. I don't rightly understand what's happening, and Esme beckons me into the caravan. Telling me to leave them be. That twins are a different breed of brother unlike any other. These same riddles Jimmy Smart talks in sometimes, when I wish he'd be plain. Inside the caravan I plead with Dreama, for her to come back to the field where she belongs. Though she'll not listen to a word of it. All the while Esme goes about her business of being mysterious. There's something in the way she moves that reminds me of the showman. Might be because after his

169

old man Bullet died Esme watched out for him. Her ways becoming his own. And we wait this way for hours until the Smart Brothers' motorcar returns, and I'm pulled out into the night myself. Bone tired and worn with worrying what's happened to him.

I'm not leaving without Dreama, I say.

I ain't asking. Just do me this one thing is all. You want me to be back at it with my brothers? Cuz I've no wish for it, Jimmy Smart says.

Where've you been all night?

Driving around is all.

Couldn't it have waited 'til morning?

My brothers ain't the waiting kind.

How'd you mean?

You're not meant to be here. On account of not being—one of us.

What about Dreama?

There's an order to things. Best I can explain, Esme outranks 'em.

I see.

I don't make the rules Eli.

They want you back turning the rides this coming Sunday?

They do. Though I've told 'em no. Now we have to leave. We'll come back for Dreama later. I promise.

Dreama says she's staying. She'll not hear me.

Reckon she feels the same way about Esme as I do about you.

And what's that? I say.

Come on. I've something to show you, Jimmy Smart says.

When I was eleven years old, I wanted to be a saint. Even after my mother tried reasoning with me. Claiming sainthood belonged to the dead. Not those living. Amused, Dreama agreed my yellow hair could be seen as saintly, though she'd been keen to know what virtue had befallen me all of a sudden. Unlike the heavy book I'd been reading out in the field, *Lives of the Saints*, I hadn't possessed any particular virtues to speak of. Instead, a knowing inside somewhere. That like the saints themselves, I was something other than I appeared to be. Different from the boys in the classroom, nor pretty as the girls with their braided hair. Something in-between. Same as the bookplates and church windows I'd gazed upon where men and women were changed by church light, becoming something else altogether. Not one thing or the other. After this realisation I'd waited for a miracle of my own. Gazed up at the moon. Wondered if Shane Wright might be such. With his ability to lift heavy things. Or later, the stones that boomed through our windowpanes. Maybe even the flood that stole my mother. Because miracles can be mysterious. Though I know none came until now. Where I find myself on the Mart at two in the morning. Jimmy Smart telling the lads who keep watch overnight to get lost. Then he introduces me to his herd of pretty horses. They snort and kick and hurtle around and around as if they've blood running through them. Something more than woodgrain. Alive with light and colour. I want to know how this can be. Why these horses appear to do his bidding, galloping as he commands them. It's more than the Italians who charmed the beasts with their clever paint. Then Jimmy Smart weaves through the horses towards me, his gaze purposeful. He helps hurl me up onto the back of a grey horse with a wild black mane. I hold on hard to the leather strap. Without music the horses are something else. Wood creaking. Cogs turning. Their muscles stretching. Like nothing else my ears have heard. Before, in Jimmy Smart's motorcar on the ride here, we drove through the cold night with nothing more to say about his brothers. Him busy smoking Woodbines, one after the other. But beside him I'd wondered where they'd taken him. Wondered too what he'd meant about how Esme feels for Dreama. What the showman feels for me. Sometimes no amount of reasoning will do. And now Jimmy Smart is hollering each time I pass by. He appears everywhere at once on account of the mirrors. Until suddenly he's behind me on the painted horse. His arms wrapped around my middle. Stirring my dick in my underclothes until I'm hard as the wood beneath me. He smells of cigarette smoke and steam. And something agreeable I don't know the name of. I ache for him to fuck me slowly in the way he does. My backside slick with his clever herbs. The heat of him inside bucking back and forth while his big palms press around my neck. Unconcerned where this desire will move me. Though for now I am content with riding this horse beneath winter sky. As Jimmy Smart promised. His mouth against my left ear. Damp and warm. Telling me things.

I want you, Jimmy Smart says.

Reckon it'll be tricky up here on this horse, I say.

Still a smartarse. What I'm trying to say is—

Go on.

These past months, here with you—they've meant more to me than everything that came before. Even those damn lions. The way I feel about you—it's baffling sometimes is all.

How'd you mean?

Don't reckon I should want you the way I do.

Because you're not like me?

No. That's not it. I am like you.

What then?

Nothing'll be the same—afterwards.

You're talking in tongues.

Don't reckon I am. Don't look at me like that. You know, some days the way you gaze at me hurts. Same as being struck in the face. Cuz the thing is, you look just like her.

Huh?

Your mother. Same coloured hair. Skin, sometimes I reckon I can peer beneath.

You fooling with me?

I ain't.

You knew my mother before the flood? I say.

No Eli. Afterwards— Jimmy Smart says.

The Brecklands at dawn are golden. Same as the savannah Ezzah and Afreen might have gazed out on in another place far away. Before they found themselves pacing back and forth across an iron cage with Jimmy Smart laid upon the roof above, hiding from himself. Though this illusion doesn't last long. Before the light shifts, slipping away, and the grass tells nothing but the truth. Brown with winter. I am here with the showman who is grim-faced. His motorcar left on the other side of a barbed wire fence we crawled beneath before following the wild path to where we shouldn't be standing. This abandoned place that once was a village. Until war came. And the Ministry of Defence claimed it for themselves. To play at killing. I am cold and my eyelids ache. Yet I've no desire to put my head against a clean bed and sleep. Not until I know the truth. Because Jimmy Smart is a liar. Surprising as a thunderclap. All along he's been here on purpose. Since the very beginning. When he tells me this, his breath blue, I want to know what exactly brought him to our field. He sighs. Recounts the summer before, finding Dreama out in the green turning in circles and nearly naked. Hoping the following time he saw her a fortnight later with Peg, she'd have no memory of their meeting. That really he'd come to find me. And when Dreama had agreed he could sleep out in black barn on a fold-out bed, he reckoned there'd be a chance to right the wrong that brought him here. Behind him the church steeple is a black thorn against sky. In the houses around us the windowpanes are black too. Nobody behind them. Empty. And I know nothing good can come from being here with the showman, while he wrestles with his wrong doing. That whatever happened will divide my life into before, and after. Like the flood water that swept over everywhere but our field. Until now I've hated the water for taking my mother, yet the ache in my stomach tells me I've laid my blame against a lie. Then, unable to gaze upon me, beneath a cruel sky, Jimmy Smart cries quietly as church. Wipes away the wet with the sleeve of his wool coat, and tells me about the time his brothers found him at the fair with a townie when he was fourteen years old. Trousers and underdrawers around his boots as the local lad sucked him. Knowing the beating would be worse than any he'd had before, he climbed into the front of their motorcar beside Tanner, Alick herding the townie into the back. The four of them drove out to the abandoned village. Pushed open heavy wooden doors ruined with bullet holes and walked the length of the church aisle. Where Jimmy Smart watched his brothers take turns fucking the townie they'd bent over a smooth pew, as he squealed and fought like a stuck pig. Afterwards, when he stopped sobbing, they made him pull up his trousers, straighten his shirt and wipe the mess from his face. Then they drove five miles back to town with the windows wound all the way down as if nothing had

175

happened. Jimmy Smart and the townie sat side by side on the warm leather back seat.

Afterwards, I wanted to hold his hand. Do something to make it right. But I did nothing. Don't even know his name, Jimmy Smart says.

It wasn't your fault, I say.

That was the first time I really understood that something was wrong with them both. I figured they'd beat me blue, finding me with an older boy like that. But they never so much as touched me. Though Tanner told me if I looked away one more time in church, it'd be me they fucked instead. And not the townie. I believed him too. Cuz he was teaching me their rules.

I hate your brothers. And those stupid rules.

I know.

Why've you brought me here?

Just cuz—

Not knowing's even worse.

Don't reckon it is. Seems to me some things are better left untold.

You're wrong. And I'm tired of these riddles. Why'd you come to the field to find me?

Cuz I wanted to. You see—I took your picture.

Where from?

Your mother's purse.

I don't understand.

The day of the flood—my brothers—

Tell me, I say.

They killed your mother, Jimmy Smart says.

Because of my sissy-sounding voice I know what it means to be held down by a man. To have him everywhere at once, his smell and sweat and power, until I have all but disappeared. It was this way with Shane Wright when I was fifteen years old. Who in the beginning pushed himself inside me with a force that left blood in my underclothes days after. Though same as the moon comes and goes, each time I came back to myself. Was able to find my reflection in a black windowpane some place. Or the oval mirror atop the chest of drawers in my bedroom. Where I'd sit and comb my yellow hair neatly, smoothing everything away. Nothing will be smooth again. Or undisturbed. Because beneath my boots my mother is buried. And Jimmy Smart helped put her there, in this abandoned village behind barbed wire. He gazes above my head. Unable to look at me. Tells me what happened quietly. Guilt is clever like that. Eating him up, like the soldiers who came home from war with gangrene. Until there's no other choice but to cut away everything that's dead. Standing here, listening to him talk, my face ruined with wet, I wonder how much of him is left. How much died the day after the flood. When he'd rode in the backseat alongside my mother, already dead in her pretty green dress. Tanner and Alick upfront. On their way to church. Her skin, he tells me, was like my own. Fine enough to peer through. This is the disappearing. That her face so similar to my own still haunts him. And suddenly I understand the restless nights laid out behind me like the tide that ebbs and flows. I want to know why they killed her. Jimmy Smart can't talk at first. Then he tells me it was during the storm. Not far from the POW camp. In the pouring rain. Because of the cigarettes, he begins. They'd wanted to buy every carton she had. But she'd told them no. Over and over. That she wanted nothing to do with the likes of them. Tanner balling his fists the way he does. Unable to hold his temper tight. A single punch and my mother down in the mud. Gone. Afterwards, they'd heaped her body in their car. And the first Jimmy Smart knew of it was the morning after the flood, when the townies were counting their dead, and his brothers took him to dig this hole. Then I clench my fist into a ball and strike Jimmy Smart on the chin. Again I hit him. Each time he steps forward, bracing himself for my fury. Now his nose is bleeding. And I want to break open the dirt, wondering if it too will flow red with my mother's blood. I turn around and around as a needle would searching for home. I want the field. To take a shovel of my own from black barn. Stride out to the middle and part the dirt until the first glint of metal glows. But what about Dreama. How will I tell her the truth. It will destroy her. Worse than the flood. Worse even than our bomb. Jimmy Smart stills me, until I am no longer turning. I say Dreama's name over again and again as if she'll somehow hear me. He promises me Esme would never let anything happen to her. I wonder if Esme and her clever cards foretold all along that my mother wasn't beneath Blackguard Sand, held deep with worn fishing nets. I'm so cold now my teeth clatter, and Jimmy Smart says we should walk back to the car before we freeze. Inside, my coat damp with weather and mud, he lights two Woodbines and passes me the spare. I take it. Smoke hurriedly. Hoping to suck some warmth from the tobacco. The glass begins to fog, Brecklands blurring, until the world outside is gone too. Twice he opens his mouth to speak, though no sound comes out, hitchhiking on his blue breath. He appears different from before. From how he was just hours ago riding the gallopers. And this scares me. I don't know why, or what exactly it means to feel what I do. How bad a person it might make me. But I can't hate him. The terrible truth is I love my mother, but Jimmy Smart more.

When you're ready, warmed up some, I'll take you home. Then I'll go to the law. Confess my wrongdoing. Cuz it's past time to tell the truth, Jimmy Smart says.

You'll hang for it. Just like Shane Wright, I say.

I will. My brothers too. It's what we deserve.

Why'd you come looking for me, afterwards?

Told you already. Your picture. I needed to know.

What—

That you'd be all right. When I found you alongside the field, and moved into black barn, I tried to tell you. But—couldn't. Don't look at me like that Eli. You know why.

What'll happen to me now?

I don't know. I wish I did.

And Dreama?

I'm sorry. I'll be sorry till my last breath.

What if I don't tell?

You can't mean that? You're not yourself on account of what's happened here.

You're wrong 'bout the truth.

How'd you mean?

What good does the truth do anyone?

It'll be hard. But I reckon in time, it'll set you and Dreama free, Jimmy Smart says.

No. My mother died in the flood. Everyone around these parts knows that, I say.

Just because I don't talk much, doesn't mean I have nothing to say. It's what I'd told Jimmy Smart on the warm river-bank that night. Air thick with gnats. Him bare-arsed and hurling himself into a situation I hadn't yet understood. Two of us hung there in cool water watching a freight train shift sand across iron tracks. Him trying to figure out our cursed field. Reasoning where such a belief might have sprung. Not knowing nothing about the bomb that fell in forty-one. And now he's apprehensive again. Believes the shock my ears have undergone at church will drive me out to the field for what lies beneath. My denying the situation hasn't helped none. On the ride home near two days before, all I'd claimed over and over was my mother drowned in the flood. That's how I find myself in Dreama's bedroom. The showman giving me hours to myself. While he disturbs the floorboards in my own room, pacing back and forth. He's hardly spoken. Just a handful of words. Him agreeing to leave the law be. For now. I turn back the heavy wool blanket. Dress quickly. My breath blue. Through the windowpane the world waits quietly. Seems to me even a scatter of blackbirds have stilled their oily wings to watch what I'll do. I go downstairs. Collect my boots from alongside the fire, where coal has warmed the leather. Tie the laces and head outside. Sky threatens snow. Then I collect my pushbike from black barn, cold handlebars hurting my hands, and pedal hard. Though I'm no match for Jimmy Smart, who's hollering like a lunatic. He pulls me from the leather seat and we tumble into a ditch, smooth with ice. For a time we gaze at one another, his face flushed with the effort. Me wondering what darkness whirls inside his head, like storm clouds gathering. All at once he's roaring with laughter. Baffling me. Until I'm laughing too. He puts rough palms against my cheeks. I reckon he might kiss me. Though he doesn't. Instead, he lifts me up and we climb out of the ditch, back onto the track.

You mind telling me where you're pedalling?
Jimmy Smart says.

To see Dreama, I say.

Figured as much. I can't allow it. I'll not have you near my brothers.

I've no such desire.

Don't be foolish Eli.

I want to know that Dreama's safe. Nothing more.

I promised she would be.

And you'd have me believe that? Without seeing for myself.

Fair enough. Will you tell her about your mother? Cuz I need to be ready for what'll come after. It won't be good.

No. I've had near two days alone to make up my mind. Enough to know no good can come from telling the truth. There's been too much told. Truth is cunning like that.

You're different.

How'd you mean?

Reckon you've finally figured out where words come from.

Thought you lied about that?

Might be I didn't, Jimmy Smart says.

You've changed me is all. I'm no longer afraid of my sissy-sounding voice, I say.

All Saint's Day is tomorrow. Jimmy smart tells me this to ease the set of my jaw. Reminding me the Mart is the first fair this season, and his brothers will likely be in Lynn guarding the gallopers from troublesome townies. Though to make certain, he drove his motorcar to a field one mile south of here. And since we've been treading this path alongside a quiet hedge, still with frost. When the way opens up, I can see the roof of Ezzah and Afreen's cage in the distance. Dreama told me the lions are buried somewhere nearby. I wonder if Jimmy Smart ever comes out here in warm weather. Puts his back against the ground. Like I do. Dreama and my mother too, before the Smart brothers killed her. I stand still. Jimmy Smart stretches out his arm and points. Over there. There's a small rise I'd not have noticed without knowing. When I gaze at him, wanting more, he shrugs and walks away. We find Dreama outside Esme's caravan, beating dirt from a rag rug. A cloud of dust hounding her. She's wrapped in a wool coat and purple shawl pulled about her yellow hair. She passes Esme the wooden stick. Takes hold of me. As if I've been in a foreign land for years. At war perhaps. Her gaze travels from boots to crown, trying to determine what's changed. A sudden ache inside startles me. Because I didn't know it would hurt to be here again. In the same way Jimmy Smart believes I resemble my mother, really Dreama does. As if the two were twins themselves. Both beautiful. Both lost to me now. When I was fourteen years old, after the man in blue swimming trunks changed me beneath the cliffs, Dreama was first to understand. Though she didn't desire me to spill my secret. To turn my cheeks hot with shame, knowing something about myself I didn't, as she brushed ladybirds from her skin. Instead, she talked about the men in her own girlhood. How little she'd cared for them. And my mother. Writing unsent letters to a man who'd died before I was born. My father. That's when Jimmy Smart tells us he'll make himself scarce. Esme goes with him. Arm in arm. They don't look back, and Dreama tells me to get beating the rug strung across a length of rope, while she lights her Woodbine. She puts her back against the caravan and blows blue smoke about. Using the palm of her spare hand to gather ash. As though she's still at our house alongside the field. I quit gazing on her, take up the stick. The cane is twisted into a pleasing swirl at the end. Coloured mainly grey and brown, I suspect the rags are torn from worn trousers. All of a sudden I consider how many men are gathered here. If Jimmy Smart's old man, Bullet, is one of them. The showman's brothers even. And I beat the rug with more force than I might otherwise. Until for a moment, Dreama has disappeared behind the muck. She tells me to steady on, before I have the whole line loose, coiling on the ground. I'm flushed from the effort. Unsteady. Dreama has me put my backside against the caravan step. Sits down herself. Takes hold of my hand. Hers a similar size to my own. Then I begin crying. Something I'm accustomed to of late. Dreama coos, and I feel like that oily bird in my mother's hand the day of the flood. Trapped. By everything I don't yet know. Though that bird was really the padlock I had forgotten to close. I wipe my face, feeling foolish. Dreama gazes ahead when she speaks. Telling me the cold hard truth.

You remember being eleven-years-old? When you wanted to be a saint? Dreama says.

I do, I say.

Knew it then. You mother did, too.

What might that be?

That you were something different—than you
appeared to be. Something that doesn't belong here.
Even more so after the flood. And those goddamn
stones.

You saying I should leave?

I am.

What about you? You all right here with Esme?

More than all right.

Field isn't the same without you.

Oh I reckon the field'll manage somehow.
Don't you?

Suppose it will. Been wondering. You still have
Adie Lovekin's pendulum?

Wear it every day.

You and Esme—you know what's coming for me?
In the future, I mean.

Some—

Like what?

He'll come back to turn the gallopers. Though I
don't need no cards or a pendulum to know that.

Jimmy Smart, you mean?

Exact same.

Might be—I love him, I say.

There's no might about it, Dreama says.

The gallopers are turning. Painted horses, three abreast, hurtle around and around. Kicking and neighing. Up and down. Townies riding their backs and hollering. While the Smart Brothers move amongst the pretty colours like herdsmen in another land. Collecting coin. Tipping wool caps. Jimmy Smart stands at the middle, alongside the engine. Steam billowing about him. He appears and disappears with each turn. He's not laid eyes on me yet. Because I'm across from the market square and glimmering lights. I've my back against this cold wall. Above the window there's a heart carved into red brick. Dreama told me a woman burned here years before. That her heart burst from her chest and left its mark. Seems to me my own heart might as well be hung up there alongside hers. If I believed such a thing. On account of the way things ended with me and Jimmy Smart the day before. Two of us stood out on the edge of our field, wondering where to begin. Me shaking more from apprehension than falling snow. Quietly coming down. Waiting for words that have no desire to come. After a big silence, he told me he'd quit the station. That his brothers won't leave him alone until he has a mind to turn the gallopers again. His face solemn with the certainty of it all. His fate sure as sunrise. Though my ears hung on to his words differently. Because what he meant was he'd done with me. The field. And sleeping in my bed. I'd been struck dumb. Not knowing how I'd failed to see it coming, like lightening five miles out. That's when he headed for the house. I'd known what for. When he came back outside his khaki canvas bag was hauled across his shoulder. Heavy with everything he owned. I'd said not one word. And that's why I've come to the Mart this night. Not to whirl around. Nor hurl coconuts. Instead, to say something I'm waiting on. Not knowing exactly what it will be. Perhaps Esme could pull the words from me with her clever cards. Dreama is likely here too. Though I've not yet gazed upon them. Hidden here. These shadows I stand amongst, while townies tire of cotton-candy and turning. Leaving the glimmer behind. I'm relieved when Jimmy Smart's brothers disappear. I suppose they'll drink beer now, until they can't hardly stand. Finally, I'm walking the fair. Ground slick with muddy boot prints. Past canvas covered stalls. Glass bowls with gold fish that hang in yellowed water. When Jimmy Smart catches sight of me, he strides forward. Restless and surprised, all at once. Tells me I shouldn't be here. There's a worn rag in his hand he's being running over the grey horse, to clean away grime. The rest of the herd are still too. As if they're grazing. Behind him the night is solemn and everywhere. I can't shift my gaze from his. He's clean-shaven now. Like the first day he came to our field. And at last, I know what I need to say.

You look like yourself again, I say.

Beard was itchy as hell. Besides, the townies don't care for it. Esme reckons it isn't fitting. How long you been here? Jimmy Smart says.

Not so long. Thing is, I wanted to know—

What?

If you're happy now?

How'd you mean?

Back here with your herd of horses. And your brothers.

You know the truth of it.

I know you're a coward—after all. Too afraid to take hold of something good. Something right in front of you. Me—

It ain't that simple Eli. And I've told you before— I'm no coward. You don't understand my world. Don't reckon you ever could.

You're wrong. I understand all of it. Even your lions. Come home. I promised you I'd never tell. And meant it too.

I can't do that.

Why not?

Cuz it's too hard to stay.

How can it be?

You're too difficult to gaze on. The guilt. I can't take it. Can't take the way I am neither. None of it. Don't—touch me.

This us over then?

I reckon it is.

I love you Jimmy Smart.

You think I don't know that?

Then—come home, I say.

Thing is Eli, this is my home, Jimmy Smart says.

August sun is everywhere. Laid on the pine tabletop. Glimmering about the place. Passing through window-panes, hung ajar to let the air inside. Though Dreama, sat across from me in her shiny slip, smoking a Woodbine, reckons it makes little difference. She reminds me of that night with Jimmy Smart. Out in his motorcar racing around the roads until we'd made our own cool wind. It's been six months since I gazed on him. Too many silent hours out at the river, beneath the iron bridge. Drifting in the green water. Writing in my notebook on the riverbank. Because I stay away from the field of late. And what lies beneath. Later, when Dreama's found what she's searching for, I'll ask her about him. Perhaps. She's here to dig out a photograph of my mother. Wearing a purple dress. Though she tells me you'd not know this from the photograph. I don't recall such a dress. Yet imagine it smells of violets. Dreama has made up her mind I should take it with me when I leave. National Service is surprising like that. Finishing my glass of water, I pour another. Hair heavy against my forehead. Suppose it'll be shorn off soon enough. I'm not sure I'll make a very good soldier. There's nothing to be done about it. My medical examination passed. Seems even my sissy-sounding voice can't keep me from a uniform. Nor do I know what I'll find out there past our field. But something. Now Dreama is stubbing out her Woodbine. She gets up. Her considering where to search next, while she ties her yellow hair into a clever knot. Her eyes the exact same colour as cornflowers. Outside Esme's motorcar is on the track. Waiting to take her home to the showpeople when she's finished here. Might be I hope she never finds that photograph. Instead, the two of us carry on like before the flood. Before Jimmy Smart. I mean to follow her into black barn, yet the music's returned again. In my head. The sound of the merry-go-round. Gallopers kicking and snorting and neighing. Dreama calls after me. Inside the barn she has already opened up a box. Her head disappeared with rummaging. I lean against a crate. Bare-chested, it's still sweltering. Before, Dreama told me I'm becoming a man. Broadening out. I've not told her about the push-ups. I count each night. Because I feel like a traitor. Wanting to be something more. A man. That thing that does their damnedest to disappear the women in this family. Then Dreama wants to know if I've forgotten what we're doing. I stride over. Lift the lid on a wooden trunk. There's a tin spinning top inside, painted with a scatter of blackbirds, I've long since tired of turning. And other childish things. I close it carefully. Collect another box and tug loose the lid. This one's stuffed with folded flowers, dresses belonging to my mother and Dreama. I wonder if her purple dress is inside. With my boot I slide the box along the ground, where it topples the fold-out bed. Jimmy Smart's. There's a sudden ache to put my back against canvas. With it, my memory of him unfolds. Hands everywhere at once. His dick distracting me. The scent of sweat and herbs and semen. Until nothing else matters. Not the water whirling the night of the flood. Not my sissy-sounding voice. Dreama startles me, her hand on my arm.

I shrug. As though what I'm remembering is nothing much at all. I want to tell her at first I believed I'd met Jimmy Smart too late. Though really, I reckon he came too early. Like a sunrise before you're finished dreaming.

You ever gonna ask me what you're waiting to know? Dreama says.

Don't suppose I am, I say.

Then I'll tell you anyway.

If you want—

He's not doing so good. Drinking—fighting—mostly with himself I reckon. He'll come out of it in time. Least that's what Esme sees.

He ever talk about me?

Doesn't say much of anything to anyone, if the truth be known.

He know about my National Service? That I'm fixing to leave here?

I told him—

I waited for him afterwards. Reckoned he'd come back after a few days. Him seeing sense. But he never did.

Same as your mother. I waited every day for a year. Watching past those broken windowpanes—hoping.

Seems to me hope does nobody any good.

Might be you're right.

You reckon that photograph's out here? I say.

We'll see, Dreama says.

With my bare back against warm dirt, hands cradling my head, I'm gazing up at the moon. Full as can be, filling up my eyes. Until I reckon light is spilling down my cheeks as tears have a mind to sometimes. Dreama left a while back. Climbed into Esme's blue motorcar and rode away. But not before holding me in her arms tightly. Her yellow hair everywhere, smelling like Woodbines and childhood. Something else I don't know the name of. Now I find myself out here in our field. Beneath, there's a bomb that fell when I was seven years old. And I'm wondering if someday, someone will finally dig it up. When I asked Dreama what'll happen now the house is empty, the field with no one to whirl around and around upon it, she sighed. Told me it'll all go on without the three of us. I believe her too. Dreama is wise like that. Wise enough to know that somewhere out in black barn there'd be a leather album, worn smooth from turning, with my mother's photograph pinned inside. I've laid the likeness on the centre of my chest. Her all pretty in purple, that's really the same colour as Jimmy Smart's grey galloper. The one we rode that night. Different from all the others. Him behind me, holding on. And suddenly I wonder if he might be in a field someplace, laid in long grass with my picture on his chest. I know it's better this way. For Dreama too. Her not ever knowing. Nothing good can come from it. And here I am, content as I've any right to be. Lying to the moon.

Reckon that might be the brightest thing I've ever gazed on, I say.

That's true, my mother says.

I can't stay long mind.

Where else do you have to be? On a night like this.

Jimmy Smart's taking me to the fair.

That so?

Uh huh.

You know he's the kind of trouble you can do without.

How'd you mean?

He'll disappear you. If you let him.

Then I won't.

You know what I'm thinking?

Dunno—

Let's go out to the river. Before I melt. Tell me you've time before the fair, my mother says.

Plenty— I say.

Acknowledgements

My deep appreciation to my publishers Sarah and Kate Beal, who continue to support my small stories with huge passion.

Thank you, Abi Fellows, Fiona Brownlee, Jim MacSweeney, and Uli Lenart.

Heartfelt thanks to my editor Matthew Bates, whose keen eye and unwavering friendship, shaped the book you find before you.

Love to my sister Kate, for reminding me where words come from. And Mark, for making it possible to write them down.